BLOOD AND DESPERATION

"Prepare to meet your god!" the leader said as he jumped in and raised the morning star to smash Conan's face. Conan twisted, nearly tearing free of the death grip on his legs, but he knew he was too slow—

Then from out of the night came a whooshing noise, almost like that of an arrow whistling but louder, and the bandit leader suddenly sprouted a fence post from the center of his back. The morning star fell and sank into the body of the dead man on Conan's legs.

Conan stared. What had entered the leader's back and pierced through to exit from his chest was no post. It was a spear, but what a spear! The leafshaped blade was longer and wider and thicker than Conan's hand, and the shaft to which it was affixed was as big around as his arm.

What kind of arm could throw a spear that big?

CONAN

THE
FORM

The Adventures of Conan
Published by Tor Books

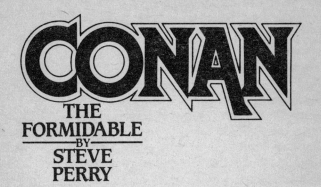

CONAN
THE FORMIDABLE
BY
STEVE PERRY

TOR®

A TOM DOHERTY ASSOCIATES BOOK
NEW YORK

CONAN THE FORMIDABLE

Copyright © 1990 by Conan Properties, Inc.

A Tor Book
Published by Tom Doherty Associates, Inc.
49 West 24th Street
New York, N.Y. 10010

Cover art by Ken Kelly

ISBN: 0-812-51377-0

First edition: November 1990
First mass market printing: August 1991

Printed in the United States of America

0 9 8 7 6 5 4 3 2 1

For Dianne, for the usual reasons
and a whole lot more; and for
John Reading and Harold Lotz and
Hopper's in the spring of '65.

ACKNOWLEDGMENTS

For help in the writing of this book, I must thank Jim Rigney, who made me do it this way, and Wanda June Alexander, who almost saved me from the mad copy editor last time.

"Those who wish to appear wise among fools, among the wise seem foolish."

—Quintilian

ONE

Along the road toward wicked Shadizar from the Karpash Mountains came the young man, a long blued-iron sword sheathed over his left hip. The lone figure loomed larger than most men; he was tall, broad of shoulder and thick of arm and leg, his skin tanned the color of dry rawhide, with flashing blue eyes, high cheekbones, and a strong chin.

Here, the sun remorselessly baked the Zamoran plateau, drawing spirals of heat from the flat, cracked ground. A hot breeze blew and spun small wind devils that twirled briefly with nowhere to go before dwindling to their dusty death.

That same sweltering breeze stirred the square-cut black mane of the young man as he paused to drink from the leathern water sack he carried. The liquid was tepid and reeked of iron and sulphur, but Conan of Cimmeria had tasted worse and been glad of it. He lowered the skin and looked around.

There was little to see. The plateau bore scant growth, a few scrubby bushes here and there. Ahead, perhaps another three hours' walk, was a rocky outcrop, not quite a foothill, but offering some trees and shade, did Conan's sharp eyes not lie.

The journey toward Shadizar had been long and treacherous, and even though the sun smote him with its hot hand, Conan was glad of the quiet desolation. Thus far he had encountered all manner of dangers from men and beasts, and things worse than either. It was his good fortune to have survived, albeit he would have done so in a somewhat better style had he been able. He wished now for a robe to reflect the bright light from his brawny frame; that would make the walk cooler and easier.

The Cimmerian laughed aloud. "Aye," he said to the empty, cooked landscape, "a robe and a horse, and a bag of gold across the fine saddle, while I am wishing!"

He took another drink of the water, plugged the skin, and started walking again. He had a fine sword, its edge sharped to razor keenness; he wore a pair of leather underbreeks, a wide belt and a purse, though this container was empty, and he had a water skin yet half full. More, he had strong legs, and sturdy feet shod in well-cut sandals. A man could do a lot worse. Conan's god was Crom the Warrior, and Crom allowed a man measures of things at birth: a certain amount of strength, this much cunning, that much wisdom. After that a man was on his own; Crom cared not for whiners, and it did not pay to call upon the god for favors.

Conan had seen Crom once. Or thought he had. He smiled at the memory. Aye. What a man did with what he was given was up to him. And what Conan had was a desire to travel to the City of Thieves to ply the trade of that metropolis and become wealthy. A few more days and he would finally arrive. Once there and laden with stolen jewels and coins, he could drink and wench and enjoy his well-earned luxury.

Until then, he would walk.

As night drew her twilight veils across the land, she allowed a welcome coolness to flow into the air. Conan found himself in the outcrop toward which he had trudged, and the road to Shadizar wound now its way through hardy evergreen trees and thicker scrub brush. He saw signs of small animals and decided he would construct several snares with which to catch his supper before making camp for the night. He had no cloak, nor had he furs to soften the ground, but it would be the work of only a few moments to make a bed of branches and aromatic needles. The evening was already cooler than the day by far, but it would not grow much more so; he had outwalked finally the frosty breath of the mountains.

It was while setting his third snare of twisted vines that the Cimmerian's keen hearing detected a noise normally foreign to the lairs of ground squirrels.

Somebody sneezed. He had never heard such a sound from a rabbit, and certainly no rabbit would follow the sneeze with a soft but definitely human curse.

Giving no sign that he had heard, Conan continued to set the snare, looping the vine over the bent sapling and locking into place the notched pegs that held the trap cocked. Alerted, however, the Cimmerian strained his ears to catch other sounds in the gathering dusk.

He was near the edge of the road, astride a narrow animal trail that disappeared into a thicket of thorny bushes. A small clearing of dry grasses lay to his left, and a stand of evergreen trees with heavy undergrowth stood across the road. It was from this last area that the sneeze had come.

As he finished the snare, Conan's ears continued their report. There came the rasp of iron against leather—a short sword or dirk being drawn—the liquid clink of chain mail and the creak of leather armor, another sneeze and a muted curse, followed by a whispered admonition for silence. This last was in a heavily accented version of the Zamoran commontongue.

So. He had unseen companions in yon trees, and from the sound of them, they had questionable intent. A friendly party would have hailed him in the open and not skulked about in hiding, drawing weapons and urging each other to silence.

Conan considered his surroundings. He would move toward the thorn bushes and put his back to them. No one would be coming from that direction.

With the Cimmerian, the thought was the deed. He strode to the bushes, turned to face the woods, and drew his broadsword. Night had not yet won her battle with day, and the sinking sun glinted from the blued blade as it sang forth from its scabbard with the tones of dry leather rubbed on cold iron. Conan gripped the handle with both hands, right over left, and swung the weapon back and forth to limber his wrists and shoulders.

"Ho, dogs of the night! Come forth and declare yourselves!"

After ten heartbeats, the bandits began moving noisily through the brush and out onto the packed dirt of the road. There were six of them, and Conan did not doubt that they were brigands. They wore the vestiges of military gear; odd collections of mail, gauntlets, and bowl-shaped brass helmets. Perhaps they had once been warriors in some army, or perhaps they had merely waylaid some poor troop and stolen the armor. Two of the men carried short and curved swords; two more held wooden spears with daggerlike points; one man bore a pair of fat knives, and the last man carried a morning star—an iron ball studded with spikes and mounted on a wooden handle as long as Conan's arm. A motley assemblage, to be sure.

The man with the morning star stepped out ahead of the others. He was short but wide and muscular, and nearly bald. He did not wear a helmet. "No need to be insulting, barbarian. We are not night dogs, but merely . . . ah . . . poor pilgrims on a journey."

Conan laughed. Was that supposed to make him put away his sword? "Pilgrims?"

"Aye, and as such, we are short of coins. Perchance would you happen to have any you could contribute to our cause?"

"No."

"Ah. Well, that sword you wave about so dangerously might be worth something. We could sell it."

"I am not disposed to give it up."

The man waved the morning star at his band. "There are six of us and but one of you. Give us the sword and whatever valuables you carry and you may leave here unharmed."

"Pardon me for not trusting you, but I think not."

"There are still six of us to your one."

"That can be changed." Conan grinned wolfishly, showing his strong white teeth.

The man with the morning star shrugged. He turned to his men. "Alas, the gods wish us to work for our living, brothers. Slay him."

The six spread out and began to move toward the Cimmerian. He watched them and assessed

6

their strengths as they came at him. The spear carriers plodded, both being fat men, and Conan ranked them low in skill. The swordsmen were young, although one walked with a limp and the other nervously shifted his grip on his weapon like a man playing a flute. If the bandit with the two knives had survived many encounters such as this with no more than those weapons, he must be fast and adept. And the leader, with the spiked iron ball, had probably become leader by besting any challengers. All of them could kill and had probably done so before, but the leader and the knifeman were the ones to be most wary of, Conan judged.

Likely they expected him to stand fast and parry their attacks, using the thorn bushes as protection for his back. That would be the most prudent and expected defense.

It was for that reason that as they formed a ragged semicircle around him, Conan screamed and leaped at the brigands.

The two spearmen were closest. Startled, they tried to back up and thrust with their spears at the same time. Neither act did they do well. The Cimmerian swung the sword and slammed the first man's spear shaft aside. He continued the stroke in a circle over his head and brought the bluediron blade down. The sharp edge sheared through the brass helmet and bit deeply into skull and brain, and the spearman dropped as if his legs had disappeared.

The other spearman turned to flee, and Conan

jerked his blade from the head of the first attacker and jumped at the man, skewering him from the side, driving the point of the sword deeply in between two ribs and through one lung and the heart. The man screamed and dropped his spear to grab the thing killing him. He lost four fingers as Conan jerked the blade free and slung blood from it into the eyes of the nervous swordsman trying to sneak behind him.

"Set's balls—!" the man began. He did not finish the curse, for Conan's sandaled foot caught him in the belly and knocked him back into the knifeman.

It was unexpected, and the knifeman thrust out with his knives in reaction, burying both to the hilt in the amazed swordsman's kidneys. The killed man fell, taking one of the knives with him.

The limping swordsman lunged at Conan, slipped, and fell onto his face. As the Cimmerian dodged back to avoid the fallen man, he in turn tripped over the first spearman.

"Crom!"

The knife wielder leaped in to gut him, but Conan snapped his blade up even while lying sprawled on his back and the tip entered the man's pubis. The man screamed girlishly, dropped his knife and clutched at himself, staggering off and out of the fray.

The limping sword carrier scrambled up and dove at the fallen Cimmerian—only to impale himself on the awaiting blued iron. Here was good luck and bad. Conan's sword buried itself in bone and was wrenched from his grip in the other man's final agony. He fell across Conan's legs and clutched them in a death grip. He was trapped!

"Prepare to meet your god!" the leader said as he jumped in and raised the morning star to smash Conan's face. Conan twisted, nearly tearing free of the death grip on his legs, but he knew he was too slow—!

Then from out of the night came a whooshing noise, almost like that of an arrow whistling but louder, and the bandit leader suddenly sprouted a fence post from the center of his back. The morning star fell and sank into the body of the dead man on Conan's legs.

Conan stared. What had entered the leader's back and pierced through to exit from his chest was no post. It was a spear, but what a spear! The leaf-shaped blade was longer and wider and thicker than Conan's hand, and the shaft to which it was affixed was as big around as his arm.

The leader fell backward, but stopped as the butt of the huge spear hit the ground. After a heartbeat, the dead bandit toppled to one side.

Conan bent and pried the dead swordsman's fingers from his leg and pulled himself free of the corpse. He stared at the bandit leader. What kind of arm could throw a spear that big, hard enough to go through a man that way?

As Conan got to his feet and looked for his sword, three forms came from the trees. In the thickening dark and at first glance, he could see that they were two men and a woman, dressed in leather and homespun wool. The men carried spears, which meant it was likely the woman had thrown the one that had killed the bandit and saved Conan. Amazing.

He stared at them in awe. They looked just like other men and women he had seen throughout his travels, save for one important difference. Even the woman, who was the smallest of the three, was easily half again Conan's own height, and probably twice his weight.

Giants. He was facing three giants.

Two

Despite his amazement, Conan recovered his sword and began wiping the gore from the blade, using the shirt of one of the dead bandits. A man who did not see to the care of his weapons did not deserve to have them.

"I owe you my life," he said to the giants.

The three spoke slowly to each other in a language Conan did not know. A moment passed. Then the woman, who had raven hair past her shoulders and a form that was unmistakably female despite her great size, turned toward the Cimmerian. She spoke to him in the same Zamoran commontongue in which he had addressed the trio.

"You fought well. You are not of the local tribes of men."

Her voice was understandably deep, but feminine. Her features, large though they were, were not unattractive, and her proportions were like those of an ordinary woman grown nearly twice normal size. Conan had seen men who were supposed to be giants, but most of those were oddly built, with thick brows and lips, and hands and feet distorted from the usual.

"I am Conan, of Cimmeria," he said, "a country far to the north of here. I journey to Shadizar." He inspected his blade for nicks and was pleased to find it free from such defects.

Another pause, and the woman turned to speak to her companions in that same language they had used earlier. After yet another long moment, she turned back toward Conan. They seemed very deliberate in their actions, he noted.

"Our village is near the road to Shadizar. Perhaps you might like to visit us?"

"Are any more of your people so . . . large as you?"

"Except for the children, we are all of like size."

Conan considered that. A village full of giants! Certainly that would be a sight to behold. Shadizar had waited this long—surely it would wait another day or two?

"Aye, a visit to your village would be worthwhile."

One of the male giants went to retrieve the woman's spear from the body of the bandit leader. The weapon came loose easily in the giant's grip; it made a noise somewhat between that of a boot being pulled from mud and a nail twisted free of wet wood. He handed it to the woman.

"That spear was well thrown," Conan said.

"I am called Teyle," she said, "and we are known as the Jatte people. I can sometimes hit my target with this—"she thumped the spear's butt on the hard ground—"but I have little strength compared to most."

Conan looked at the wound in the chest of the dead bandit, a hole into which he could easily have inserted his hand. The strongest normal man would have difficulty lifting and hurling the weapon that had done such damage, and this giant woman claimed to be a weakling. What the Jatte people lacked in speed, they most definitely made up for in strength.

"Have you food?" Teyle asked. "We have wine and cheese and meat. You are welcome to share it."

"I am in your debt already," Conan said.

Teyle looked at the dead bandits. "These were carrion eaters," she said. "They deserved no better than death. It is you who have saved us the effort of removing most of them."

Well, that was true enough, though he had done it for his own reasons. And such work did make a man hungry.

"Wine, you said?"

"Aye."

Conan slept well, his dreams fueled by the free and excellent wine, his rest made better by knowing a trio of stalwart giants shared his campsite.

Surely they meant him no harm, when they could have easily slain him at the same time they slew the bandit leader.

When dawn streaked the clear skies with its first glimmers, the Cimmerian arose feeling much refreshed. Here was another adventure, but one that seemed without the dangers of his most recent travels. A village of giants need fear little, and he was their guest.

As they set out on the road after a filling breakfast, Teyle, the only one of the trio with whom he could converse, told Conan something of the Jatte's history.

"Three hundred years past," she said, "our ancestors were brought to life by a wizard who needed strong backs for construction of his castle. He was a benevolent magician, and when the work was done, he gave the Jatte their freedom. Since that time, we have lived more or less peacefully in the village where first we began."

It seemed to Conan that a cloud of emotion passed over Teyle's face when she spoke this last sentence, but he did not press her on it.

They walked in silence for some hours, save for slow conversations among the Jatte trio that Teyle did not bother to translate for the Cimmerian.

Around midday they came to a narrow path that wound down a cleft in the rocks to their right. Conan followed the three along this trail until it came to parallel a small stream lined with willow trees and cattails. Another hour's walk took them into thicker vegetation, and yet another hour brought them to the beginnings of a swamp. Here the ground turned mushy and the trees grew taller, forming a canopy that kept out the sun's light in many places. A stray beam lanced through here and there, but the buzz of insects and the slosh of the water were largely undisturbed by the sun that had rested so heavily upon Conan only the previous day.

The path had long since vanished, but the giants seemed to know just where to step to avoid sinking into the increasing mire. This was not a journey the Cimmerian would like to undertake the first time alone, for patches of quicksand and mud were apparent nearly everywhere, and serpents slithered across their track more than once, some of the snakes being as big around as Conan's legs and thrice the length of a man. As long as he was following the giants, however, he did not worry. Where they could put their huge feet and enormous weight, he had no fear of treading.

It was while they halted on a relatively dry patch of the swamp to eat that Conan's keen ears detected a strange chittering noise in the distance. It was almost like that of a ditch frog after a hard rain.

The giants noticed the sound as well. The taller of the two males snarled and said, "Vargs!" He spat on the damp ground.

Conan turned to Teyle. "Vargs?"

The woman nodded, "Swamp-dwelling beasts. They are like Jatte but very small. Smaller even than you. They have green, mottled skins, they file their teeth to points, and they are the worst kind of savages. They roam in packs and they . . . eat Jatte flesh."

Conan considered that. A creature that ate giants might also be disposed to eat human flesh. Unconsciously, his right hand drifted over to touch the handle of his broadsword.

"They are cowards," she continued, "and attack only if they outnumber us a dozen to one. Probably we shall not be bothered by them."

Conan nodded. Nevertheless, he would stay alert.

They followed the twisting trail through the swamp. Several times the Cimmerian was warned against a misstep by his companions, and he realized that the village of the giants was unlikely to be visited by accident. Nay, even if someone knew where it lay and was bent on reaching it, the journey would be perilous at best. Conan had a sharp eye for detail, and his memory of trails once traveled would stay clear for long periods. But even so, this was not a trip he would wish to make without great care as to where to put his feet.

It was late afternoon before they broke free of the swamp and found themselves at the edge of the Jatte village.

It was an impressive sight.

The houses were made mostly of wood, with thatch roofs, and even the smallest of them was large by men's standards. A number of the Jatte moved and worked in Conan's view. Here, women pounded grain for flour; there, men cut logs for firewood or construction; yonder, children played at mock battles. It made the Cimmerian feel as if he were but child-sized, as indeed here he was; even those children who had only begun their earliest changes into adults were as large or larger than Conan. He had never seen the like.

Some of the villagers stopped what they were doing and came to greet the returning trio, and those that came looked at Conan with curious eyes. They chattered at each other in their own tongue, and Conan heard his name mentioned by Teyle.

After a few moments, Teyle and her two companions led Conan to a large structure near the center of the village. Close to the entrance were a boy and a girl. Both were slightly larger than Conan, though he judged their ages at around thirteen winters. They wore spun-wool shirts and short kilts, and their feet were shod in mottled green leather boots that rose halfway to their knees. Each had hair the color of Teyle's, and there seemed to be a family resemblance.

Teyle pointed to the boy. "This is Oren." The boy smiled. "And this is Morja, his twin sister. They are my younger siblings."

Conan nodded at the children.

"A fine specimen, Teyle!" the boys said.

Conan looked at the giant woman. "Specimen?"

"I have taught them something of the language you use," she said. "But they often speak it badly."

Conan accepted this; true, the young often did things badly.

"My father is inside," she said. "He wishes to meet you."

"How can he know of my arrival?"

"The twins would have told him."

17

Inside, the large building was dim, lit only by the numerous windows cut through the walls and left open to the outside. A particularly large giant, nearly twice Conan's own height, stood next to what appeared to be a solid but empty cage near the center of the room. There were tables and chairs set around the perimeter of the enclosure, as well as large baskets of woven straw reeds here and there.

"Ho, Teyle!" the giant called.

"Ho, Father."

Conan and the woman left the others at the doorway and walked toward her father. He wore a dark beard flecked with gray, but was naked save for a tanned animal hide wrapped around his hips and extending to his knees. His chest and shoulders and arms were mounded with heavy muscle, and his skin was tanned darker than Conan's. Conan got the impression that this giant could break him in half with no more effort than a man would expend in breaking a broomstick.

"This is the man Conan," she said, "who slew five of the men bandits at the plateau outcrop. My father, Raseri, chief of the Jatte, and also the tribe's shaman."

"Five bandits, eh?" Raseri said, his voice booming loudly in the enclosed space. "Excellent, my daughter! A fine specimen you have brought me!"

There was that word again, and this time Conan did not think it was used accidentally. He had a sudden stab of worry, and he started to turn to face Teyle.

He saw her hand, knotted into a great fist that made his own seem tiny, blurring toward his head. "I am sorry," she said.

Before even his quick reflexes could protect him, the world flashed red and yellow and went black as Conan's consciousness fled his body.

THREE

The wagon wound along the High Corinthian Road over the packed snow of the pass into Zamora. The conveyance laboring under the frigid breath of the mountains was constructed mostly of wood, built long and wide, with high sides and a peaked roof of taut and heavy cloth that protected the inside from many of the vagaries of weather. The tall wooden wheels, six in number, were bound by bands of iron, the hubs packed thick with black grease, the spokes wrapped in strips of aged green copper for extra strength. Along the baseboard a vitruvian design had been carved deeply into the wood, though the intricate scrollwork had been bleached as gray as the rest of the aged timber by the sun's unforgiving gaze.

The vehicle's size was such that it was necessarily restricted to the larger roads, and the speed achieved by its six harnessed oxen was slow at best.

On the front of the wagon, before a cloth curtain that screened the interior, sat a cowled figure whose face lay in deep shadow. He held the reins connected to the oxen in gloved hands.

After a moment a second figure emerged from the wagon's bowels and sat next to the driver. This second man was fair, with hair the color of fresh straw, his face clean-shaven and handsome by most standards. He wore a gray woolen robe similar to the driver's. He slapped the driver on the back of one shoulder. "Ho, Penz. Dake would have you stop so that we may prepare a meal."

A wordless growl issued from under the hood.

The blond man grinned, showing beautiful teeth. "Ah, hairy one, you are too dour. You need to enjoy life more!"

With that, the man reached up and grabbed the cowl covering his companion's face and jerked the cloth back, uncovering the one called Penz.

Penz snarled and swung his gloved fist at the other, hard. The backhanded gesture was powerful, and the force of the strike knocked the blond man from the seat, to fall nearly his own height to the packed snow of the road. Penz reached for his cowl and pulled it back into place, but not before the reason for his distress was obvious to any who might be there to see.

Penz had the face of a beast. Of a wolf.

Where a man would have a nose, Penz had a muzzle, ending in a snout. When he showed his teeth in rage, they were long in front, pointed, designed for tearing flesh. And, except for the snout and the deep-set eyes, his entire face was covered with coarse, stiff hair. More like fur than human hair.

As the oxen drifted to a stop, Penz made as if to leap from the wagon onto the fallen man when a powerful voice cut through the air's hard chill like the lash of a whip.

"Penz! Hold!"

The man with the face of a wolf froze as if slammed on the head by a hammer.

Through the curtain came a third man. He was the opposite of the man struggling to rise in the snow next to the wagon. The third man's skin was swarthy, his hair the color of a flock of ravens; a long mustache dangled well below his squarish chin. He was wide under his robe, and the muscles of his forearms where they cleared the sleeves danced with power as he flexed his fingers into huge fists.

The blonde meanwhile came to his feet. "I will smash your furry face!"

The swarthy man glared at the blonde. "Silence, Kreg!"

The enraged Kreg glared at the speaker, then found cause to look down at the damp spots on his robe. He brushed at the snow still clinging to him and did not speak against the command to hold his tongue.

To Penz, the swarthy man said, "You are not to strike Kreg. Punishment is mine, do you understand? I am the master here!"

Penz nodded.

"Say it!"

The wolfman managed an understandable reply. "Dake is the master."

"Good," Dake said. And with that, he swung one of his huge fists and clouted Penz in the chest, knocking him from the wagon and into the grinning Kreg. The blonde's grin vanished as the heavy form of the wolfman knocked him flat into the snow again.

"And *you* are not to taunt Penz again," Dake said. He moved back into the wagon, leaving the two men lying on the cold ground.

Inside, the wagon appeared larger than it did from without. There were benches upon which to sit, latched cabinets built into the sides, and enough sleeping space for a dozen large men. Tro the catwoman and Sab the four-armed man sat looking apprehensively at Dake as he returned to the padded bench that was reserved for his use. He scowled at them. No one in all of Corinthia or Zamora, or even in Koth, had a collection of oddities such as his, but Dake was not satisfied. Tro was as feline as Penz was wolfish. Her body was very womanlike under the fur, however, and more than a few men had paid for the privilege of enjoying the catwoman. Dake had used her himself, though of late he had less desire that way.

Sab's second set of arms was smaller than the first, but both sets were functional, and he always drew those willing to pay to see him. The crowds had thinned somewhat of recent days though, and Dake knew he needed something better with which to draw paying audiences. And something mayhaps bigger.

Between his small skills as a mage and his collection of freaks he would not starve, but Dake's ambition was to be the chief entertainer of a king somewhere, with enough money to indulge his main desire: to breed and grow stranger and stranger creatures, to become a master of the grotesque, with dozens, maybe hundreds, of monsters, things never before seen by the eyes of men. There were wizards who could produce such with a wave of one hand, he knew, but Dake's magicks were of a small order, and it was not within him to rise to the heights of those wonder-workers. No, he could conjure little things, but it was not his to be a great wizard. He could, however, become a great collector.

Rumor had it that there was a race of giants somewhere off the road to Shadizar. And the same tale-tellers spoke of a dwarfish folk, no taller than small children when fully grown, also living nearby. Dwarves were common, but these tiny men were said to be the color of tree frogs. To add two such creatures to his collection would greatly augment Dake's chances of finding a patron, so it was with this intent that he traveled toward the City of Thieves. He even had a rough map, purchased from a fine example of drunken tavern scum at a run-down inn just inside the wall of the city of Opkothard. The man had been down to drinking dreg wine, and a bottle of more of the same had bought his treasure. For a few coppers, Dake had a location that might produce a specimen of great value to him. Of course there was always the chance that the map was a fake and not even worth the sheepskin upon which it had been enscribed, but Dake did not think it so. He had a nose for such things, and the carefully maintained map, folded and refolded hundreds of times over years, had the look of authenticity. Were this so, it would be worth a vineyard and cheap at a dozen times the price he had tendered.

The thought of besting another, even a total sot, in a business deal and the possibility of attaining a wealthy patron cheered Dake somewhat, enough so that he felt a rush of pleasure that changed into another kind of desire.

He smiled at the catwoman and nodded toward the big bed that he alone was allowed to use—save for times when he invited another to join him there. As he did now.

Tro sighed and stood, moving toward the bed.

Dake went to join her, and he laughed as he saw Sab turn his face away. The four-armed man was in love with the catwoman, as she was with him, though neither knew that Dake was aware of this.

Too bad. It did not matter what they wanted. They were not people, they were oddities. It mattered only what Dake desired, for he was the master, was he not?

When the sun had made two full circuits of the skies and the moon had bathed the world in her light twice also, the wagon arrived at the place where its occupants would have to depart from the well-made road.

The wolfman stood next to the wagon. Dake stood next to Penz, and Kreg next to him, observing a winding path that descended a rocky decline toward what appeared to be a stream a ways below.

"There," Penz said, pointed one gloved finger toward the south.

"You are certain?" Dake asked.

"Aye. See there in the distance the thick green? That would be the swamp."

Dake unfolded the map and looked at it again. He had another copy of it, one he had made with his own hand in the event this one was lost or damaged. It seemed that Penz was correct.

The dark man said, "We shall have to find a place to conceal the wagon. That patch of forest half an hour's walk back should do it."

Kreg said, "What of the oxen?"

"They can roam free, they will not wander far. And they will come when I call them." Dake waved his hand, curling the fingers in a come-hither gesture. A geas to call domestic beasts was hardly a major spell, and one Dake could perform without much ado. Though he had not been born a magician, he had shrewdly learned over the years that sometimes even mages could fall upon hard times and that during those periods they could be induced to sell some of their smaller spells, were the price offered high enough.

"Should not we leave someone to guard the wagon?" Kreg asked.

"No." Dake could also put a repellent conjure upon the wagon so that any passersby unskilled in the arts would find themselves uncomfortably near vomiting in the immediate vicinity. Such a magical ward could hardly keep a witch or wizard of any talent at bay, but then, a mage of any real power would hardly need or want a wagon, even such a fine one as Dake's. "No, we shall all go down the path together. I may need your talents in securing our new companions."

Penz went to turn the wagon and start it back toward its place of concealment. Dake stood for a moment gazing out at the distant trees that likely stood rooted in a swamp. It had been some years since he had graced Shadizar with his presence, but he knew there were wealthy men there who would enjoy the notoriety of being the sponsor of Dake's menagerie . . . especially if Dake could obtain a true giant and a new kind of dwarf to add to it.

Already the possibilities of interbreeding stimulated the mage's imagination: a giant catman or woman? A dwarf wolfman with green fur? A four-armed giant or dwarf, perhaps? True, certain species did not always conceive when bred with other species, but there were spells that could aid in such couplings. Dake knew some of the easier conjurations, and he knew that with sufficient gold, he could purchase others.

He turned and climbed up onto the back of the wagon, smiling as he did so.

The possibilities were many, and rife with excitement.

FOUR

Conan awoke to find himself inside a cage.

The Cimmerian had a pain in his head and stiffness in his muscles. The cause of the latter appeared to have come from lying on the floor of an odd cage; it took a moment for his mind to recall the reason for the former. The memory, when it came, was not pleasant.

The woman giant had struck him while his attention had been elsewhere. And as for her claim of being a weakling, Conan was unconvinced. No man had ever struck him that hard.

His situation did not look promising. Conan sat and rubbed at the sore spot on his head. He looked around. His sword and scabbard were gone, but save for that, he had been left with his clothes, belt, and purse. He had flint and steel and punk, and therefore the ability to make fire. This oversight was a mistake on the part of his captors.

The cage, which he had not had time to observe closely before, was constructed of a hard white substance that for a moment defeated his attempts to identify. The odd-shaped bars and rods were of varying sizes, woven together in strange patterns and sealed at the joints by a greenish material, obviously a kind of glue. Attempts to pick away the seals with a fingernail and the firesteel proved no more effective than an equal effort would be on stone. And when he struck the white rods with a knuckle, they gave back a tone that was metallic, as if he had tapped on bars of bronze.

Bones.

It came to Conan suddenly that the rods and bars of his cage were made of bone. And judging from the lengths of the longer ones, the bones had come from creatures considerably larger than was he.

"Ah, awake, I see."

Conan twisted and spotted the giant whom Teyle had identified as her father, Raseri, standing behind the cage.

"Tell me," the giant continued, "have you any idea as to the situation in which you find yourself?"

Conan was not disposed to be talkative, but the other had the advantage of him. It might not be wise to irritate a giant who had you in a cage. He said, "I am in a cage made of bone that is exceedingly hard, bones taken from those of your kind, I suspect. I cannot guess as to the reasons why. Perhaps you people are cannibals."

The giant laughed, a deep and booming sound that bounced from the walls of the room. "Very good! You are correct about the cage. Our Creator, knowing we would need special structures were we to be useful to him, gave us stronger bones than little men have. And your conjecture as to our being cannibals is a good theory, given your circumstances, but wrong. Unlike the Vargs, we are not savages; rather, we are natural philosophers."

Conan did not know the term and he did not speak. The more knowledge the giant gave him, the better Conan's chances of escape.

"I see by your expression that you are unfamiliar with our doctrine. Natural philosophy is the study of the world and that which is within it. We seek to know all things about all things."

The giant moved closer toward the cage, until he came to stand his own height away. He looked down at Conan. "If we are to survive in a world where we are greatly outnumbered by men who hate and fear us, we must know everything there is to know about our enemies. Therefore you have become a specimen for our study."

"I am no scholar," Conan said. "I can tell you little."

"Ah, but you are not the first to occupy that cage.

We have . . . studied those you call scholars. We know that there are many different kinds of little men, just as there are of us. We have need to question a warrior, one from another land."

"I do not need to be in a cage to answer questions."

"Ah, but I am afraid you must be. Some of the questions are physical ones, and painful."

Conan stared at Raseri. For a moment the Cimmerian's flashing blue eyes grew smoky. They meant to torture him. Well. When the cage door was opened, he would see how strong they were against his most potent rage. He knew that his speed was greater than theirs and if he could somehow get to his sword—there it was, propped against the wall behind the giant—then he would see how hard the flesh of giants was when compared to a sharp blade. Better certainly to die with sword in hand than to submit meekly to torture. Crom welcomed warriors but had little use for men who would not fight. Since it seemed that Conan was soon to join his god, best if he did so accompanied by as many of his enemies as he could bring with him. There were worse things than dying; dying badly was one.

The swamps were thick and full of dense vegetation, scummy pools, and treacherous footing. The sun's rays managed to pierce the canopy in only a few places, and the resulting darkness, even at midday, gave the air a constant gloom.

Perhaps this gloom was why Kreg strayed from

the narrow path down which Tro's sure feet led the group. The fair-haired man began to sink into the ubiquitous sludge.

"Help!"

Dake shook his head in disgust. To Penz he said, "Pull him out."

The man-wolf nodded once and removed the coil of rope looped over his shoulder. He uncoiled the end of the hemp carefully and held it in his left hand as he made ready to toss the rope to Kreg.

"Hurry, you hairy fool!" By this time Kreg had sunk to his thighs in the muck and his struggles to free himself only caused him to settle faster.

Dake sighed. Kreg was loyal to a fault, but more than a little stupid. For a man trapped in a mire that would swallow him to hurl insults at his rescuer demonstrated a lack of wit. Did not Dake command Penz to save him, then the wolfman, no doubt grinning all the while, would certainly allow Kreg to sink to his bubbly death. One did not want one's assistant to be too smart or too ambitious and therefore dangerous, but perhaps Kreg's loyalty was overly offset by his dullness.

Penz hurled the rope. Since Kreg was but a few spans away, the circles of heavy hemp uncoiled only a little and the main mass of the line struck the trapped man solidly, hitting him hard on the face and chest.

"Ow! Set curse you!"

Dake could not see Penz's face, hidden as it was

by his cowl, but he felt certain that the man wore a wolfish smile.

Around them, the swamp buzzed with insects. Kreg's legs made sucking noises as Penz hauled him free of the entrapping ooze. When Kreg was halfway free, Penz jerked the rope a little too hard and Kreg fell forward onto his face, splattering mud in all directions.

Behind Dake, both Tro and Sab laughed.

Kreg dragged himself back onto the path and stood shaking with rage. He glared at Penz. "You off-balanced me on purpose!" He pulled a long dagger from his belt. "I will have your ears for this!"

"Put the knife away," Dake commanded.

Kreg, too stupid to realize his own danger, turned to glare at his master. "You saw what he did!"

"And I saw that it was you who strayed from the path. Next time I shall let you sink!"

Penz began methodically recoiling the rope.

Kreg shook with rage, but he put the dagger back into its sheath.

Dake turned away. One day these two would try seriously to kill each other. Penz was too valuable to lose, and if Kreg did not mend his anger, then he would have to be dealt with. Assistants were easy to come by, wolfmen were not. It was sad, but loyalty could not make up for everything.

And there were more pressing matters to be settled first. Dwarves to find, and giants to capture.

As if in answer to his thought there came a strange sound from the depths of the swamp, a sing-song drone unlike anything the mage had ever heard before.

"What is that?" Kreg asked.

"Let us proceed forward and find out," Dake said.

Deep in the bowels of the swamp, where no human had ever ventured, past the quickest of killer sands and through trees that sometimes grew as thick as a palisade wall, lay the home of the southernmost tribe of Vargs. In the clearing next to the cold soaking pool, Fosull, the leader of the tribe, picked a bit of flesh from between his pointed front teeth with a sharpened fingernail, then chewed thoughtfully on the bit of gristle. He was the tallest and best-knit of his people, nearly a quarter as high as one of the Jatte, and he could run faster and climb quicker than Vargs half his age. His mottled green skin had a few wrinkles here and there, and his eyes were perhaps not quite as sharp as they had been a dozen summers past, but no one dared challenge him for the leadership yet, not even his oldest son, Vilken, though that day would not be long in coming. The boy needed a bit more seasoning, but Fosull would have no problem in stepping aside in another summer or two to allow Vilken to do the hard work of leader while he, Fosull, attended to his nine wives and accepted the due of a retired rather than a dead leader.

As Fosull prepared to remove his breechskin before stepping into the pool, Brack, one of the trail watchers, came running up. "Ho, Leader!"

Fosull sucked his teeth and affected a bored look. "The day is warm and I am about to enjoy the water. What is it?"

"Trespassers, Leader."

"Jatte?"

"No. Outswamp men. And odd ones."

"How odd?"

"One has four arms. Another the face of a dire beast. There is a catlike female. The other two are ordinary."

"Interesting. And where did you see this group?"

"On the lower Turtle Trail."

Fosull considered this information. True, the outswamp men were not nearly so tasty as were the Jatte; then again, food was food, and better outswamp men than no men at all. The Varg diet of late had been confined mostly to swamp pigs and assorted rodents, so five outswamp men, even if odd ones, would be worth a feast. The soak pool would have to wait.

"Very well. Assemble the warriors at high Turtle. We shall take the intruders at the mossback turn."

"My leader."

Brack sprinted off into the bush. Fosull went to collect his spear where it stood propped against the lush vinelimb tree that overhung the pool. Perhaps the oddity of the intruders would add to their flavor?

One could hope.

* * *

Conan had been alone in the cage for most of the morning. His eyes still smarted from the smelly liquid that Raseri had splashed upon him before leaving. The giant had hurled the contents of a smallish wooden bowl at him, and the resulting odor reminded Conan of a dead rat left three days in the hot sun. Other than a mild stinging in his eyes, the Cimmerian had noted no ill effects from the stinking shower. Raseri had watched him for a moment after the spray, nodded to himself, then departed.

This was like no torture of which Conan had ever heard.

Teyle entered the structure and walked toward the cage. Conan glared at her but did not speak.

"The *koughmn* caused you little distress, I see," she said.

He held his tongue.

"You must understand that I bear you no ill will," she said. "I was charged by my father to obtain a specimen of little-man warrior, and you were unfortunate enough to happen along."

Conan found small consolation in this. He still did not speak.

"We are few and the little men are many," she continued. "To survive, we must know our enemies. Surely you can understand this?"

"Until I arrived here, I was not your enemy," Conan finally said.

"But your kind are. I regret that I had to trick you, but I had my duty."

"I would be more forgiving were you to unfasten the door to this cage and release me."

"Alas, it cannot be so. I only wanted you to know that your being here is not personal."

"It seems that I am to die in a cage under the hand of your kind, so you will forgive me if I take it personally."

Teyle had nothing to say to this, and she turned and walked away.

Conan looked again at the cage. Where he judged the door began and ended, the joints were sealed with that same greenish glue as were the rest of the bars. He had already determined that the substance was impervious to being scratched by his flint or steel, and that it would not burn. Neither would the metallic bones take fire.

Carefully the Cimmerian pitted his muscles against each of the bones forming his prison, trying to find a weak spot. In one corner he came across a single bone the length and approximate thickness of his arm; it creaked a little as he tugged on it. Removing it would not allow an opening large enough to permit escape, but it would give him a possible tool with which to pry. Too, he could use the bone as a club. Should Raseri come close enough, he could try to shatter his skull; mayhaps he could throw the makeshift club and effect some damage. Better something than nothing.

Conan gripped one end of the loose bone and pulled, putting his back and shoulders fully into the effort. The strut creaked and seemed to give somewhat. He relaxed a moment, then tugged again.

The thought of smashing Raseri gave Conan reason to smile grimly. Killing one of the giants would go at least a short way toward making up for not having seen the trap.

He kept working at the bone.

It was not as if he had anything better to do at the moment.

FIVE

The attack upon his party took Dake by surprise. On the cusp of one moment, the five of them were slogging through a marshy clearing; on the cusp of the next moment, a horde of screaming little green men brandishing spears streamed out of the thick brush that lay ahead.

In that instant, which seemed to stretch slowly like hot resin pulled from tree bark, Dake realized that he and his collection of oddities would be overwhelmed by the sheer number of attackers. There must be at least a score of them. He had to do something quickly were he and his to survive.

Dake hurriedly spoke the words of a spell. The space behind him shimmered; there came a clap like thunder, and of an instant there stood behind him a gigantic red demon. Three times the height of a tall man, the thing flashed cruel fangs and slashed at the turgid swamp air with claws that appeared easily capable of disemboweling an ox.

The dwarves skidded and slid to a halt almost as one.

Dake waved at the demon and it took a step forward.

The little green creatures broke and ran back toward the cover of the swamp, chattering at each other and calling no doubt on their gods for protection.

Dake smiled. The demon was, of course, no more than an illusion, with less substance than the smoke of a campfire. Certainly it appeared real, and who in his right mind would care to get close enough to be able to say otherwise?

As the dwarves fled, Dake called to Penz, "Catch me one!"

The wolfman nodded and trotted forward, uncoiling his rope. Penz kept a sliding noose formed on one end of the rope, and now he twirled this over his head and threw it so that it encircled one of the fleeing dwarves. Penz pulled the rope taut, and the sudden jerk snapped the green dwarf from his feet. The little man sat hard upon the squishy ground.

Well. If catching a giant were this easy, they would be back on the road to Shadizar before much longer.

The green dwarf struggled, but Penz kept the rope tight so that there was not enough play for the captured one to regain his footing. Dake hurried toward his new prize.

The demon faded into nothingness as its creator withdrew his attention from it. He had a real spell to cast, the mage did, and the threat of attack was gone.

As the dwarf moved toward Penz, seeking to slacken his bondage, Dake spoke the words of his most effective enchantment. The holding spell settled over the dwarf almost visibly, so that he ceased struggling and became calm.

"You are mine now," Dake said. "You cannot escape my geas."

Whether the little man understood him or not Dake could not say, but he was now bound—as were the other members of the mage's collection—by a magical net that rendered him helpless to harm or flee from his new master.

"Loose the rope," Dake commanded Penz.

The wolfman did so.

The new thrall looked at his captors. Dake made an upward motion with one hand, indicating that the dwarf should arise. The little man did so, albeit somewhat reluctantly. He tried to fight the spell—they all did that at first—but Dake only smiled again. This was the one magic of real power that he currently used, and it worked exceedingly well. Better to be able to do one thing well than nothing at all, and his trick had served him unfailingly thus far.

"Let us continue," Dake said.

"Wh-what of this one's brothers?" Kreg asked.

"You saw how they reacted to the demon. They will not bother us again."

Kreg looked doubtful, but he was not one to

gainsay his master. The troops, newly enlarged by one, moved on.

Behind Raseri, four male giants entered the room that had become Conan's prison. Each of the four carried a long, straight staff. These sticks appeared to be at least the length and thickness of a giant's spear shaft. At a signal from Raseri, the giants gathered around the cage, one on each side.

Raseri spoke a single word and the four stepped toward the cage and lowered their staves.

From behind Conan, the first staff was thrust into his cage, hard. Conan felt the motion somehow and twisted to avoid being poked. He clubbed at the staff with one knotted hand, the hammer of his fist connecting solidly and battering the stick downward, but before he could further react, a second staff jabbed him in the back.

The Cimmerian grunted and absorbed the blow, dodging to one side as a third attack entered his domain.

The cage was of sufficient height for him to stand, but any upward leap would bring Conan's head into contact with the top of the prison, so he was limited to moving from side to side or dropping. Unfortunately, there was no one place in the cage where he could avoid all four cudgels.

A staff hit him a glancing blow on the thigh, knocking him to one side, where another poke took him in the belly.

Conan's mind scrambled for a way to protect himself. These four were too strong; he would be battered to death within a few moments did he not do something!

A near miss gave him a chance. He grabbed and tried to pull one of the staves from the grasp of its wielder. The giant pulled the stick back with such force that Conan lost his grip.

With death riding his shoulder, Conan saw another small hope.

The dimensions of the cage were such that while he could not avoid all four staves, were he to stand in the middle of one side pressed against the bars, three of the attackers would not be able to reach him without moving; thus far, they had kept their places. Of course such a move would render him more open to the attacker on that side, but better one than four.

He leaped as the nearest giant thrust his staff at his belly, turned so that the end of the weapon slid by, barely touching him, and slammed into the bone wall, shoulder and hip first. Conan grabbed the extended staff with both hands, scissored his legs around the wood and locked his ankles together, pulled the staff to his chest, clutching at it with hands, arms, thighs, and ankles.

Even the giant could not hold a man of Conan's weight extended at arms' length on the end of a stick. Conan crashed to the floor of the cage, pulling the staff from the surprised giant's grip.

Instantly the Cimmerian was up. He had a weapon!

He shifted the heavy staff as he came to a crouch, and thrust it back at its former owner with all the power he possessed.

Guided by Conan's hasty but well-aimed jab, the staff caught the giant squarely on the forehead. The sound was like that of a mallet striking a tent peg. The startled giant's eyes rolled back in his head and he dropped to his knees, then fell onto his right side. The cage shook from the fallen giant's impact with the ground.

Conan pivoted and pulled the staff halfway back into the cage. It was too heavy for him to swing properly, even had he the room, but perhaps he could land a few blows before the others beat him senseless. He grinned wolfishly.

"Excellent!" Raseri said, clapping his hands. He spoke another foreign phrase and the three remaining giants lowered their staves.

Conan regarded the giant leader. His blood sang with rage and he would have liked to attack, but despite his small victory, he was still caged and at Raseri's mercy.

"Most resourceful," Raseri said. "And given the nature of the attack, the only possible response."

"Free me from this cage and I will demonstrate other responses," Conan said, hefting the staff.

Raseri smiled. "Oh, no, of course not. We have many more tests for you. Surrender the staff."

"Nay, I would keep it. Take it if you can."

"I cannot allow you to keep it, for it might be used as a lever. The *ekad* glue is hard, but you are strong and might be able to wrench an opening by which you could escape."

Conan did not move.

"I can have them batter you again," Raseri said, waving at the trio.

"Better to die fighting than to submit like a goat to the slaughter."

"Ah. A warrior's code. Very good. But it is not yet time for you to die. Tender the staff."

"No."

With that, Raseri reached into a pouch at his belt. His hand was closed when he removed it.

Conan shifted his stance. He lifted the staff, balanced it in his hand, and drew back his arm. It had no point, but hurled with sufficient force, it might do some damage. A blunt spear was better than none at all.

Before the Cimmerian could make his desperate cast, however, Raseri flung the contents of his hand at the caged man. A black powder shimmered in the air. Conan leaped to the side but could not avoid the dust. He made to hold his breath, but an acrid stink told him he had already inhaled some of the powder. His vision swam and blurred, and he felt his legs weaken. With the last of his strength, Conan threw the staff, but already the drug had stolen his power. The staff sailed from the cage and clattered harmlessly at Raseri's feet.

Once again the darkness claimed Conan for its own.

Raseri was elated.

The specimen his daughter had collected was perhaps the best upon which he had ever experimented. This outland small man was brave, strong, and clever. There was much to be learned from him.

The leader of the Jatte looked up from his writing table at the unconscious captive in his cage. His personal elation was tempered by the knowledge that small men like this one represented a great danger for his kind. The local specimens had not demonstrated such abilities or defiance. Most of them had been so terrified at the mere existence of such as the Jatte that their resistance had been almost nil. Most had died quickly, most had done so pleading. Were they the norm, then the Jatte could prosper without undue worry.

But ... if this outlander was more representative of what the small men could do and be, there was indeed a problem. Sooner or later the Jatte would become known to the outside world. Already a few small men had somehow managed to overcome the swamp, and even the Vargs, to arrive at the village, though none had left. It was but a matter of time before others managed the task.

Teyle had no stomach for his experiments, but she was too softhearted. What she saw as torture, Raseri saw as only necessity. She saw the little men as people and not as the threat that Raseri knew they would someday become. She could picture things only in the moment, while Raseri had to take the long view. Ten seasons or a hundred seasons might pass without incident, but what of his children's children? Without a means to understand and defend themselves, their future might be lost. Raseri had long ago given up his regret at doing what must be done to ensure the survival of his people. Life was, after all, difficult, and the gods helped those most who were willing to help themselves. Conan there in the cage would die, but his death would be of benefit to the Jatte. That was all that was important. Knowledge was strength—the more, the better.

He turned back to his parchment and began to outline the results of the most recent test. The pictures necessary for the task were most intricate, and it took a great deal of care to inscribe them properly. It would do no good to put them down if later they were to be misinterpreted. Raseri bent to his purpose.

Deep in the swamp, in the ceremonial clearing where sometimes he presided over the ritual slaughter of captured enemies, Fosull gathered his shaken warriors about him. The sun revealed himself here, and his light showed more than Fosull cared to see. Even the Vargs, accustomed to fighting Jatte thrice their size, had been terrified at the appearance of the red giant, who made the Jatte seem small. A being from the depths of nightmare it had been, and the warriors still spoke of it breathlessly.

"Have you ever imagined such a monster?"

"Those teeth could crunch a turtle's shell!"

"It was looking right at *me*—!"

"Silence!" Fosull commanded. "You babble like children."

"But you yourself saw it, Fosull—"

"I saw that it was big, but only one and we were many. And my warriors ran like mice from a tree cat!"

"What would you have had us do? Die under

those talons? This was a magical being, not of this world!"

Fosull did not speak to that, for that much was true enough. He had seen the monster shimmer into life from the air, and no Varg magic could begin to match such a thing. The shaman could cure chills and sometimes heal a barren womb with his spells, but no shaman had ever been able to create monsters from nothingness. Maybe a spear would be as a thorn prick to such a beast.

"We will have a war council," Fosull said. "And decide how to deal with these outswamp men. Where is my son? Vilken? To me."

After a moment the Vargs realized that the chief's oldest male child was not among them.

"Vilken! Where are you?"

But Vilken was not to be found. Fosull's belly clenched as he realized that he had not seen his son since the attack on the small band and its demon protector.

Could it be that Vilken, his heir and the next chief of the Vargs, had been caught by the monster? That Vilken was now no more than a half-digested meal for that hideous red thing from the bowels of Gehanna?

Fosull shuddered at the thought.

Shaken though he was, Fosull was chief, and showing his emotions to his warriors would belittle him. He cast the worry from himself. "We will have a war council."

"The outswamp men may escape," one of the warriors said.

"Nay, they will not. They move toward the Jatte

village," Fosull said. "Even their demon cannot overcome all the Jatte, I will wager. And if they escape from the giants, we will be waiting for them when they return."

"But how can we fight such a thing?"

"There are ways," Fosull said. "There are always ways."

SIX

Dake's group, less one, crouched in the thick brush a short way off the trail. A thicket of fan-shaped plants concealed them from the eyes of any passersby upon the trail, and it would take more than a casual intent to wander through the vegetation accidently, dense as it was. Dake's clothing had suffered from an encounter with a thorn bush not ten spans away, and he did not envy anyone else who might chance upon that needle-tipped plant.

Penz, whose lightness and fleetness of foot matched well his wolfish appearance, made his way quietly back to where the rest of them lay hidden. The wolfman arrived and squatted next to Dake.

"Well?" the mage said.

"The village is but ten minutes from here."

Ah! Then the rumor was true. "Did you see any of them alone?"

"Nay. I saw only groups, working."

Dake mulled that over. His plan for securing a giant was simple enough. If they could find one alone, keep it distracted so that he could get close enough to enspell it with his obedience geas, the task would be done. Size should not affect the magic, but distance from the subject did. Unless he was close to the quarry, the spell would not work. Better it was a giant who would not be missed for a time, a woodcutter away from prying eyes, or a hunter or gatherer. That way they could be a goodly distance away from the village before anyone started searching for the captive. Dake did not fancy having to fight an entire horde of giants, and he suspected his demon illusion would fare less well with them than it had with the green dwarves.

The master of freaks glanced at his latest acquisition as he thought this. Nasty little brute, his teeth all filed to points that way, his skin near the shade of a spotted tree frog, dark green splotches against a lighter hue of the same color. Unlike most dwarves, this one's head and hands and feet were in proportion to his body. Save for his size, the little green creature was built much like any ordinary man. Still, Dake was most pleased with the capture, and in itself, the froggish one alone was worth the trip. But back to the object of the original quest.

"Just how large are these giants?" Dake asked.

Penz spread his arms wide and glanced at his hands each in turn. "Nearly two spans, the men. The women are somewhat shorter."

Almost twice the height of a man. Excellent!

"Very well. We shall move closer and await our opportunity to ensnare one of them."

Visions of a sinecure danced in Dake's thoughts. Wealthy patrons would fight each other for the right to sponsor his breeding program, and he would become a man of substance and standing, respected for his talents and skills. Ah, yes!

When Conan awoke this time, the room was quiet. He sensed a presence behind him, and he sat up in the cold and uncomfortable cage of bones and turned to see who watched him.

Two children stood there.

Conan recognized them as the twins Teyle had named upon his arrival at the village. Her younger siblings, she had said. Assuming she had not lied about this, and there was no reason Conan saw for her to have done so, they were called Oren and Morja.

"Why do you stare?" Conan asked. "Have you never seen a normal-sized man before?"

"We are normal-sized," Oren said. "You are one of the small men."

"And we have seen only a few such as you," Morja added. "Mostly they did not survive our father's experiments for long."

Conan was not comforted by this knowledge.

"You shall not last long either," Oren said.

53

Came then the sound of someone's approaching footfalls.

"Father comes!"

The twins looked around in panic. "We must hide!" Morja said.

Against the far wall, away from the door, was a collection of large baskets. The two giant children ran toward these and secreted themselves behind the containers.

After a moment Raseri entered the room and approached Conan, obviously looking for something. Or someone.

"I seek my youngest children," he said. "A boy and a girl of thirteen seasons. Have you seen them?"

Conan was a warrior, and as such, normally straightforward and forthright in his speech. There was no dishonor, however, in lying to a captor who intended to torture you to death. Anything a man could do to thwart an enemy in such a situation seemed perfectly valid to the Cimmerian. "Nay," he said. "No one has been here save yourself."

Raseri muttered something under his breath and turned away. After a moment he was gone again.

Oren and Morja peeked from behind their hiding place, then slipped from concealment and approached the caged man.

"We are forbidden to enter here whenever our father conducts his experiments on the small men or the Vargs," the girl said. "To do so and be caught means that we would be beaten and restricted to the children's huts for a full cycle of the moon. Why did you not tell him we were here?"

"Why should I? He is my enemy. I owe him nothing but resistance."

"Come," Oren said. "Best we leave before our father returns." The boy started toward the doorway.

Morja said, "As children of our father, we must be considered your enemies as well. You could have caused us much suffering."

"I do not make war on children."

"We are as large as you and likely as strong," the boy said. "I would wager I can throw a spear as far as any small man!"

"Even so," Conan said.

The girl turned to follow her brother, but as she did, she spoke, softly so that Oren could not hear. "Thank you, small man."

"I am called Conan."

"Then thank you, Conan."

After they were gone, he returned to the cage slat upon which he had expended no small effort. The bone felt as if it had a slight bit more give to it than when he had begun working on it. He did not know how much time he might have left, but he had no better options to explore at the moment. Better to die trying something, anything, than to sit and wait helplessly for fate to claim him.

Grasping the strut, Conan tugged at it, relaxed, pulled again, rested, then strained against the iron-hard bone yet one more time. Apparently Raseri did not intend to feed him or allow him water, doubtless to test his ability to do without. Did he not escape soon, hunger and thirst would begin to weaken him. Whatever happened, Conan did not intend to die parched or of starvation. A man could effect his own end in many ways, especially in a cage as unyielding as this one, or as long as he could reach his own flesh with his teeth.

He hoped, however, it would not come to that. Perhaps Raseri would bring back others to torment him with sticks again. That way he could meet his end on his feet and in combat, as a warrior should.

The night was alive with sounds. Bats chittered, frogs croaked, hunting cats cried in the distance. Insects buzzed and hummed in the fetid darkness, and small, scaled things splashed in the myriad bodies of stagnant and scummy water all around the six who lay hidden near the Jatte village.

Dake slapped at an insect biting the side of his neck. Curse this swamp! There were more crawling and flying vermin here than ever he had seen anywhere. Did they not secure their quarry soon, they would be bled dry by the clouds of mosquitoes and other pests that inhabited the darkness!

No opportunity had yet presented itself to catch one of the giants. None had left the village, at least not that the mage or his entourage could ascertain.

Dake considered several options. Moving about in the night would offer a mixed blessing. On the one hand, they would be much less likely to be seen. On the other hand, the risks associated with the bungling about in unfamiliar surroundings in the dark were high. Morning might bring the chance that a solitary worker would leave the village, or it might not.

Another small denizen tried to steal Dake's blood, this time from the back of one bare hand. He crushed the insect with a quick slap.

In the end, the noxious living and biting clouds of pests decided it for Dake. There were no guards posted; the villagers obviously felt safe in their homes. They would steal into the village while the giants slept and secure a captive. Between Penz and Tro's animal senses, they should be able to travel in the dark without losing the path. When morning came, the troop could be far away from the village.

Dake motioned for the others to gather in closer so that he could explain his plan.

In the darkness of his prison Conan heard a faint crack as he pulled on the bar of his cage. The bone shifted in his hands; 'twas only a hairsbreadth, but enough to bring a wide grin to the Cimmerian's face. He could not see the joint where the green glue coated the whiteness, but a quick exploration with his fingertips told the tale. The coating was like unto the hardness of rock, but it was also brittle. The constant small flexing of the bone under the adhesive had been enough to cause a tracery of fine lines to appear beneath Conan's touch.

Cracks. Faint ones to be sure, but definitely there.

Conan redoubled his efforts. There came to his ears further splintery sounds. Chips of the hardened glue popped away from the joint, unseen in the dark but felt as they struck his hands and wrists. The bone now had more slack in it. He shifted his grip toward the joining, which had begun to squeak and make a grinding sound with each tug. It was definitely moving more readily!

With a suddenness, the bone wrenched loose at one end.

Conan uttered a short, sharp laugh, and without pausing, pivoted the free end of the bone upward. The opposite end, still anchored, cracked the surrounding glue, shattering it as a smith's hammer might shatter a small stone.

The bone was quite heavy in Conan's grip as he lifted it. As long as his arm and thicker than his wrist, the thing made a formidable club. Conan swung it back and forth, continuing to smile at the pitch-black room. More important, the bone was a tool. With it he could pry at other joints, mayhaps even shatter the glue by pounding at it. The gap he had created was not nearly large enough to allow him to escape, but given a few hours unimpeded, Conan felt certain he could free himself. Once he was out of the cage, the Jatte would not recapture him so easily as they had taken him. He still had his flint and steel, and yon baskets against the wall would make fine tinder. With this building—and perhaps a few others—in flames, the giants would be too busy to worry about him. 'Twould serve them right if the entire village burned to the ground.

Conan raised the club and smashed it downward. Glue chips flew.

* * *

In the arms of night, and further hidden beneath the safety of a thorn thicket, the Vargs slept, save for the watch and Fosull. The chief sat just outside the wicked bushes with his spear across his lap. He brooded. He had told his warriors that he had a plan for combating the giant red demon and that he would reveal it when the time was ripe.

In truth, Fosull had no such plan. Oh, he had an *idea.* When the great demon had sprung forth, Fosull had been looking at one of the outswamp men, a darkish, swarthy person with black hair on his head and dangling from his face. This one was evidently the leader, and it was he who had summoned the monster. Put a few spears through that one before the demon was called and perhaps the others could not raise the hideous thing. Or, even if the demon did arise, mayhap the slaying of its master would cause it to turn on the others.

As strategy and tactics went, this idea was not particularly well formed. If, however, attacking the demon seemed foolish, this at least seemed less so to Fosull. Were it not his son who was held by the outswamp men, he would have been disposed to allow the group to leave unmolested, rather than risk the unknown dangers. But a chief who did not try to free his heir would hardly remain chief for long. Vargs respected strength, and they had little patience with any kind of weakness. Already his warriors had halfway convinced themselves that they had not really been afraid of the demon, merely startled. For Fosull to admit that the monster had frightened him would be his downfall.

And there was Vilken to consider. The boy was his oldest son, after all, and while he had half a dozen other sons and nearly that many daughters, a Varg did not let his first-born simply be taken—not by anyone, not by another tribe of Vargs, not by Jatte, not even by a monster from the pit. Some recovery effort had to be made.

Fosull sighed and rolled his spear back and forth with his fingertips. At first light they would move toward the Jatte village and see what was to be seen. And if the idea he had did not work, well, everyone had to die eventually. If not one day, then on another. The gods would decide.

Perhaps he should offer up a few words to the gods, so that their thoughts might favor him in the coming battle. It might do no good, as often his entreaties seemed to fall upon deaf ears; then again, it certainly could not hurt.

The gods always decided one way or another, did they not? If a few well-chosen words could sway them in a given direction, a Varg would be foolish not to utter them.

The chief of the Vargs went to find a prayer rock.

SEVEN

Dake the freakmaster led his force carefully and quietly into the village of the giants. The newest of his collection, the little green man, had reluctantly supplied Dake with his name, delivered in a thickly accented but understandable variation of the local dialect. Vilken, he was called, and while the dwarf moved with reluctance, Dake saw at once that the nearness of the giants excited him. When Dake questioned Vilken about this, the answer was simple enough:

"We eat them, when we can catch them."

Dake lifted an eyebrow, but said nothing. How wasteful. Then again, he supposed, were there a large number of giants available to the outside world, the ones he planned to command would be lessened in value. That would hardly do.

"There," Dake said, pointing. "That house."

"Why that one?" Kreg asked.

What a fool. What difference did it make? Dake did not bother himself to answer his assistant.

They approached the structure. The wolfman and the catwoman kept watch as Dake and Kreg moved toward the door, followed by four-armed Sab and the green Vilken. Dake saw their shadows dance across the wall of the huge house.

The freakmaster frowned. Dancing shadows? That was wrong!

He became aware of several things almost at the same instant: The scene before him was growing brighter and seemingly orange in color; there came a crackling sound from behind, and also a strong smell of smoke in the air.

Dake spun in a half turn.

Behind them a building was on fire. Even as Dake registered this, the entire roof blossomed into flame with a deep *whuff* and the night became as bright as day.

And the night also came to life with the startled cries of a village full of giants.

Escaping from the cage provided Conan with one of his most satisfying experiences. In life, failure was to be expected at times, but failing to try, even when faced with a situation that seemed hopeless, was the worst failure of all. Every battle produced victors and vanquished, and that was the way of things; there was no dishonor in losing an honest fight. It was only in giving up when any chance still existed for winning that a man truly lost.

As the blows of his makeshift hammer shattered the final obstacle to his freedom, Conan laughed aloud. His days at the knee of his blacksmith father had not gone without producing some knowledge. Conan suspected that his father would have admired his skill as the third slat was knocked from the cage of giants' bones. Without pause, the Cimmerian wriggled through the gap and hurried through the dark toward where his sword stood propped against the wall.

Once he had buckled the sheathed blade around his hips, Conan felt better.

He moved to the baskets where the children had earlier hidden from their father. Squatting next to the containers of woven, dry reed, Conan drew hot sparks from his flint with the chunks of worn steel. The basket under the shower of tiny stars began to smolder. With the application of tiny puffs of air from Conan's pursed lips, the reed quickly took flame. In another few moments the entire collection of baskets blazed, filling the room with light and heat and smoke.

Conan felt better still as he paused long enough to watch the flames begin to lick at the wood of the wall behind it, then to greedily consume the thatch of the roof above.

The blued-iron sword sang its razor-edged hum as he snatched it from the leather scabbard and then ran toward the door. No other man would ever again occupy a cage in this building.

Grinning with satisfaction at having escaped from an enemy, the young man darted outside into the cool, safe arms of the night.

* * *

Even though he was still sitting outside the protection of the thorn bushes under which his warriors sheltered, Fosull had surrendered to a light and troubled slumber. The leader of the Vargs was startled from this fitful sleep by the shout of the watch.

Fosull rubbed at his eyes. "What is this bellowing about?"

"Fire, my leader! From the direction of the Jatte village!"

Fosull came to his feet and stared. Orange flickers painted the low night clouds in the distance. Yes, something was aflame over that way, and a large fire it was, too.

"Up!" Fosull yelled. "Awaken! To me!"

He felt a thrill of excitement rush through him. Trouble at the Jatte village could only benefit the Vargs. Maybe the fire might even provide a succulent roast or two! "Hurry, fools! The gods smile upon us and frown upon our enemies! Hurry!"

So much for his plan, Dake thought, as he led the others hurrying for the cover of a small structure behind the house they had intended to enter.

This smaller house was large enough to hold all six of his party, and at first Dake thought it was a storage shed. As the last of them entered the place, though, the stench within told a different story.

"Gah," Kreg said, wrinkling his nose. "We have found a giant's nightchamber!"

"Silence, fool!" Dake whispered. "Someone may hear you, and nightchambers do not speak!"

The mage peered through the door at the burning building. A number of the village's inhabitants had gathered to fight the fire and were hurling buckets of water onto the flames.

After his initial panic, Dake realized that this event might work in their favor. Everyone in the village would be concerned with the fire. What better time to collect a specimen? The fire had a good grip on its prey. At the very least, that one building would succumb to its hot talons and smoky fangs; it would be hours burning.

"Everybody out," Dake ordered.

"But—but the fire!" Kreg said.

"It will keep their attention, idiot. We shall collect our giant and be gone. The fire has done half our work. Hurry!"

The six made their way around the village, using the flame-created shadows of buildings to cover their moves.

Most of the men in the village fought the burning. A pair of enormous living chains led from a well to the fire, and buckets of water danced along the first line toward the building, then back along the second to the well. Those who were not in either line gathered in knots of five or ten, calling encouragement as they watched.

Gods curse them! He needed one alone!

"Find me one by himself!" Dake said.

"There stands one," Kreg said a moment later. "But it is only a woman."

Dake turned to look in the direction his assistant pointed to. A woman? A giant woman would be as good as a man, would she not? Maybe better. He could breed her perhaps. Breeding a giant man with a normal-sized woman might be a problem, but the other way around would be easier.

"Good. Circle around to her left, and if she starts to look in my direction, attract her attention."

Kreg obeyed, and Dake moved in toward his quarry.

She was too entranced by the fire to notice her stalkers until the last instant. Something alarmed her and she started to turn, but she did not manage it before Dake finished the words of his spell. She stood frozen, staring at him, unable to make even a whisper of alarm.

Dake almost laughed aloud. He had done it! He had captured a giant!

Time to depart, he thought. He hurriedly so ordered his thralls away from the frenetic activity.

As the seven moved quickly from the conflagration, they were startled to see a pair of normal-sized men come toward them out of the darkness. No, not normal men, Dake realized, but giant children!

Some god must want this venture to succeed, the mage thought. He was not one to look askance upon such a gift from a god. He quickly spoke the words of the geas yet again. Taken unaware, the children struggled, but their efforts were useless. Once again Dake's spell wove its unbreakable net, and the two young giants came into his power. Not one giant, but three! True, it would take some time for these latter two to grow to full size, but Dake could wait. And with a male and two females, he certainly had enough breeding stock with which to raise others.

Dake turned to the catwoman. "Lead us out of here, Tro. And be quick about it."

Nine figures hurried from the light of the fire and out of the village toward the swamp.

In the chaos of the burning building, Conan was tempted to stay and test his blade on a giant or two, but he knew that such a risk was unwarranted. Only a fool would attack an entire village of giants alone. The harsh land of Cimmeria did not allow many fools to reach maturity, and Conan did not count himself among those slackwits who might have somehow cheated death. He had escaped and destroyed his prison, along with the giant's precious writings about what he called natural philosophy. While he would have cheerfully cut Raseri into bloody tatters, it was not worth the risk of trying to find him in the midst of all the confusion. Giants ran this way and that, yelling, scooping water, and trying to douse the fire. Light danced, casting weird shadows, and smoke and steam boiled, making the night smell of steam and burning wood together.

Aye, he would slay Raseri, but this was not the best of times to do so. Plus, that sleep powder was tricky, and the giant leader likely had more of it in his pouch, along with who knew what else.

Nay, he thought as he slipped into the swamp, better to count himself lucky and now schooled somewhat better in the ways of the world. He would be more careful in the future about trusting people, be they his kind or giants. Crom might forgive a man a mistake once; repeating the error would likely draw the god's anger. The lesson was cheap enough, considering how costly it could have been.

Conan had enough to do as he tried to recall the treacherous path by which he had come to this place. Retracing it in the night would be no small accomplishment either. There, by that large-boled fern, he remembered that the path went that way. . . .

The distant fire cast yet enough light for him to see the trail. And more than enough illumination to reveal the sudden appearance of a dozen little men half his size, brandishing spears and showing pointed teeth that gleamed whitely against their dark faces.

Crom! What was this?

The sounds issuing from the giants' village grew fainter as Dake and his captives followed the cat-woman's lead into the swamp. Dake was elated. Even the insects seemed less bothersome; perhaps they had been drawn to the fire and consumed. By the time any pursuit might be initiated, he and his troop would be halfway to the wagon. Another few days would see them nearing Shadizar, and fame and fortune. Ah, life was good!

Conan would have retreated had there been any haven to hand. Behind him lay the village, and he had no intention of ever returning there. To either side the swamp spawned patches of deadly mire that would suck a man to his death. Ahead were the spear-carrying dwarves. None of the choices appealed, but Conan realized there was only one that he could make.

He lifted his sword. The dwarves seemed as surprised to see him as he them. His one chance lay in hacking through before they could gather their wits. He charged, screaming.

Half of the spear carriers scattered immediately, darting off the trail into the swamp. The others were slow to react. One, a bit braver or more foolish or both, hurled himself at Conan and thrust his spear at the Cimmerian's groin.

Conan twisted, swung his sword, and cut the spear's shaft cleanly. The force of the slash against the spear knocked the dwarf aside.

A second attacker jabbed at Conan, and the obsidian point of the short spear tore a shallow furrow over Conan's left hip. The Cimmerian chopped downward with his blade, and the edge bit the attacker's neck. The blur of iron passed through the rubbery padding between bones and lopped the head from the body. The dying head screamed without sound.

Never pausing, Conan leaped, his sandaled foot using the next crouching dwarf as a springboard, and flew half his own height into the air, hurtling over yet another startled dwarf, who could only watch him fly by in amazement.

Then he was past the milling horde, still on the trail, and running as fast as he could. With that ability to recall trails, Conan managed to keep his pace for some distance before he misstepped and stumbled. He fell, and at that same instant a short spear passed over him and thudded into a tree two spans away.

Conan scrambled up, regained the path, and continued to put distance between himself and the dwarves. Apparently that last-thrown spear was the extent of their pursuit, at least for the moment. He did not hear the thumps of small feet behind him; neither did the startled cries of the dwarves seem to be drawing nearer.

Giants, and then dwarves. The world, Conan realized, was full of mystery.

EIGHT

Tro's eyes equaled those of any night cat, and she led Dake and his enthralled group unerringly through the darkness along the swampy trail. What missteps she might have failed to see were spotted by Penz, whose distant kin and kith had also mastered the night. Between the two of them, the risks were minimal. The group did not run, but it moved briskly and at a pace no normal-sighted man could possibly manage without chancing the quicksand's slow death.

Whether the Vargs and the Jatte could see better than could men was not something Dake knew.

The mage was tired, but the thought of capture by either the dwarves or the giants fueled his steps, and where he went, his thralls had no choice but to accompany him.

Kreg was not under the spell that draped the others, however. "Can we not stop and rest for a moment?" he asked. "Surely they cannot pursue us, save but slowly?"

Dake shook his head. "We do not know that for certain."

"Why not ask the freaks?"

Dake slowed his pace. On occasion Kreg astounded him by making such simple yet profound statements, proffering reason that certainly should have come to Dake's own mind, but had not. Dake did not compliment his assistant on his wit; that was not his way. Compliments were useless unless there was something to be gained. He merely nodded and moved closer to the giant female.

"What is your name?" Dake spoke in the same tongue in which he had communicated with the little green man.

The woman, who was dressed in a simple homespun shift, appeared to try to fight the spell in which she was trapped. Her arm muscles bunched into tense knots. Her face tightened from the strain, and she shook her head from side to side, her hair whipping out like a dark cloud. Her efforts were to no avail of course. After a moment of struggling, she said, nearly spitting the words, "I am called Teyle."

"Can your people follow us along this trail in the dark?"

Another small time of trying to withstand his magic ensued. "Yes, but—" She bit off the rest of the reply, having met his question directly.

Dake grinned. He had had some experience with these matters. "Can they match our speed?"

"No."

"At what pace can they follow compared to ours?"

"Much slower."

His grin widened. Dake thought it unlikely that anyone would notice the missing trio before the fire was either quenched or done feasting upon the building. But even if someone did, it seemed there was little danger of being caught from behind.

Dake turned toward the dwarf and asked him the same questions. The little one had apparently accepted his lot and did not resist as he said that the Vargs could not follow quickly in the darkness either. And that was assuming they would try, believing that Dake could field a demon.

Stopping presented little risk. "Hold," Dake said to the troop. "We will rest a moment."

The group halted.

Dake turned once again toward Teyle. "Remove your garment," he said.

This time the fight to resist took longer, but in the end the giant woman did as she was told.

The moon and starlight that filtered through the canopy of trees was dim, but enough to reveal that the woman was most comely. Unlike some misshaped giants born of normal parents, Teyle was built like a woman of Dake's own kind, albeit much larger. Her form was shapely; she had melon-sized and firm breasts, wide and womanly hips, and muscular, but definitely feminine, arms and legs.

"Turn around."

Teyle obeyed.

Yes, Dake mused, this one was as attractive from behind as from the front, with nary a splotch upon her perfect form. She would produce excellent offspring; she had the body for it.

What those offspring might be was another matter.

"Put your clothing back on."

Teyle again obeyed, but this time much faster.

Dake could not tell if she had blushed. He turned, however, and noticed that the giant boy was staring at the woman as she dressed. Dake could not see his expression clearly. Was that some interest on his face? Perhaps he was old enough to breed?

"Move along," the mage ordered. "We want to be well away from here when dawn finds us."

The troop started down the path once again.

Dake laughed softly to himself. They were well ahead of any pursuit, and would be much more so by first light. Once they reached the wagon, they would be able to maintain that lead, for aided by a small spell, the transport could easily move at the pace of a man on foot, even a giant. Upon reaching civilization, the giants and dwarves, if they bothered to follow that far, would have to cease their chase. They would hardly keep their lives or their freedom long if they continued, whether they caught up with Dake or not.

Dake laughed again, pleased with himself. Fame

was only a matter of time. There were no obstacles in his path now, and none likely to be, he thought.

Conan moved along the twisty path at a steady if slow pace, his keen eyes searching for places he remembered. Trees and thick bushes loomed in the night, shadowy and indistinct, and while the swamp was cooler than it had been in the day, it was no less damp. Insects buzzed past with hums and high-pitched whines. Though his vision was sharper than that of most men he had known, the darkness required that he take special care. Signs that were easily visible in daylight were sometimes well concealed by the night's ebon cloak. Several times he had started to put his weight down upon places that would not support him, only to be saved by his quick reflexes. To slacken in his alertness could well be fatal.

The Cimmerian detected no signs of either giants or the small green men as he wound his way through the mire. Aside from that single thrown spear immediately after his encounter with the Vargs, no indications of followers had reached his senses.

He considered stopping long enough to make a torch with which to light his path, and thereby increase his speed, but decided that the risk might prove more than the aid. True, he would be able to move faster could he see better; but true also that a man carrying a flaming brand in the dark is all too visible. And a man who sat within the light of a campfire could not see into the night, being blinded by the nearness of flame. In the dark Conan was more or less concealed, and he preferred it that way. No, he would continue to grope his way along. When dawn stretched and touched the world, he could increase his pace.

Conan was both hungry and thirsty, and he did risk pausing long enough to drink from a small and sluggish stream that burbled near the trail at one turning. The water was surprisingly sweet and it refreshed the fleeing man greatly. His belly growled, complaining from lack of food, but Conan ignored it. He could, he knew, go several days without eating, and it was far better to be hungry than captured. Or dead.

Conan moved along the treacherous path, putting ever greater distance between himself and the Jatte village. An occasional break in the trees revealed orange flickers against the distant sky. These glimpses of the fire's continued life brought smiles to the Cimmerian's face.

Would, he thought, that the entire village caught flame and perished. 'Twould certainly serve them right.

Raseri ordered his people back from the burning building when it became evident that the structure could not be saved. The captured man was within, as were a number of scrolls and other items of value that he hated to lose, but there was no help for it.

The chief and shaman of the Jatte directed his firefighters to turn their efforts to the buildings closest to the one inflamed, to prevent spread of the raging blaze. Buckets of water began to splash upon the roofs and walls of those structures most likely to catch an errant spark. Within moments the drenchings had wet down all of the houses close to the fire. Heat brought forth clouds of steam, but more water was sloshed onto the drying walls to replace that stolen by the fire's breath.

Hours passed before the encircled fire began to dim. No longer free to feast, the fiery beast ate the last of its meal, unable to reach far enough to affect the surrounding structures. Like an old man, the fire grew feeble, sending up showers of sparks as a support post collapsed here and there, threatening to begin anew as the posts took flame, but impotent to go any farther. Now the buckets of water brought hissing groans from the failing creature of heat and light. Its time was almost over.

Raseri watched as the flames and heat died, leaving only smoldering spots and glowing red coals in its stead.

Miraculously, the cage of bone had escaped destruction. It stood alone in the circle of what had been a building, blackened by the heat and soot, canted slightly to one side as if a heavy weight had pressed down upon it, but still whole.

As the heat further decreased, Raseri was able to approach the cage. He expected to see the charred remains of the warrior, either sprawled upon the bottom slats or lying in roasted chunks beneath the cage. A pity. The man had shown promise of lasting longer than any other captive had ever—

By the Great Sun above!"

Raseri could feel the heat through the soles of his sandals as he trod upon the hot coals, but he ignored the smoke coming from his footgear as he ran toward the cage.

There was no sign of the body.

The captured man was *gone!*

Raseri stood staring at the empty cage. Abruptly one of his smoking sandals scorched and took flame. The giant cursed and jumped, then ran from the burned compound to cooler ground. He stamped his foot and extinguished the leather, bent and pulled both of the hot sandals from his feet, then cursed again.

The man had escaped. And the cause of the fire now seemed most obvious. The Creator curse him to the end of infinity!

Raseri turned to look at his people, who were watching him in puzzlement. The chief of the Jatte shook his head. Done was done; the building could not be brought back. How the little man had managed to free himself was a question that could be put only to him—had he not perished in the swamp, which Raseri thought to be likely. Still, they would have to be certain. If by some miracle this Conan had managed to stay to the trail and survive, he could not be allowed to return to others of his kind. The whereabouts of the Jatte village might be suspected by some on the outside, but none who had actually seen it could be allowed to go free to speak of it. The small men could not threaten that about which they did not know.

Night was waning; false dawn approached in front of his more truthful brother. At first light they would have to seek out the escapee and recapture him.

Raseri turned toward a young Jatte male. "Ready the hellhounds!"

The youth looked puzzled.

"The captive has escaped the fire and fled," Raseri said. "He must be tracked and caught."

The shaman looked around. Teyle had a bond with the hellhounds; she could control them better than any man in the village. "Teyle!" he called out loudly.

His daughter did not answer. Nor, as he found out within a few moments, would she respond. She was gone, and with her, the twins.

What kind of sorceror was this Conan, to escape the cage and to take Raseri's three favorite children?

"Bring the hellhounds!"

Far enough into the swamp and sufficiently away from the Jatte village to feel safe, the Vargs followed in confusion, and none were more addled than Fosull.

The chief of the Vargs stood leaning against a thick-boled tree, the smooth bark cool against his skin. His men had dragged three downed warriors away from the perimeter of the Jatte village, the three slain by a maddened creature that could be nothing other than one of the outswamp men. Another Varg was injured to the extent that he, too, would likely be making the journey to meet his ancestors at any moment.

Who was that man? None of the Vargs who had seen the party of outswamp men—and that included Fosull himself—had recognized the attacker. Her had burst into their midst and carved a bloody path through them, running away at a speed that would surely send him into the sandy grip of death.

"My leader!"

Fosull turned toward the warrior who called. "What is it?"

"The Jatte. They have released the hellhounds!"

As if to emphasize the warrior's words, there came the skin-pebbling howl of one of the monsters, a sound closer to a greatcat's scream than that of a wolf.

By the Great Forest God! Hellhounds! "Quickly, to the warrens!"

"What of the bodies of our comrades?"

"Leave them! They might slow the hellhounds."

But even as Fosull spoke, one of the faster of the Jatte's killer beasts bounded along the trail, foamy drool dripping from its fanged jaws.

The first glimmerings of dawn had only just begun, but there was more than enough light to see the hound clearly. Large it was, twice the size of Fosull, and while it might or might not claim hell as its birthplace, it bore little resemblance to any creature ever born of dog.

The thing paused as it arrived in the clearing,

giving the Vargs a better view of their doom. The beast's head was squarish, like unto a bear, with deep-set black eyes and flaring twin pits for a nose. Teeth it had many of, long and sharp for rending its prey, and tiny round ears to the sides of its ugly head. The hellhound's body was wolverine-like, but covered in a thick reddish fur, and its feet were wide, clawed and flat, big enough that it could use them like paddles in the swamp. A hellhound could swim with equal ease through water or quicksand, and any prey stupid enough to think to escape off-side the trail would make a quickly fatal mistake.

Fosull readied his speak for a cast. Were it simply the one, his Vargs could prevail, for they had successfully fought single hellhounds before. But with others following and his troops already weakened and in disarray, it would appear as if the battle were lost. The Jatte seldom loosed the hounds, for the warrens were protected by poisonous stakes that even the beasts could not surmount. But in the open. . . .

The hellhound sniffed the air, the sound loud in the suddenly quiet clearing. Then, after a moment that seemed to stretch as long as any Fosull had ever endured, the hellhound turned and bounded off.

Fosull stood staring at the disappearing monster.

What in the name of any god—?

The remainder of the hellhound pack, at least another seven or eight of them, streamed past, following the lead beast.

Fosull continued to stare stupidly at the pack as

it bayed and growled, moving away from him and his startled troops. Even after they were long past, he held his spear ready for what he had thought to be his last throw.

Finally he lowered his weapon. The hellhounds were not after the Vargs. That much was clear. But . . . who *were* they chasing?

In an instant the answer came to him. The out-swamp man, the one who had killed three of the Vargs. The Jatte were after him! Somehow that one must be connected to the others, those who had taken Fosull's son. They had set fire to the Jatte lodge, with the giant cage therein, and now the Jatte sought them.

Of the other outswamp men there was no sign; they must have taken another trail, but of a moment Fosull was convinced that the band who controlled the demon was also gone from the village.

If the hellhounds caught them, then Vilken would be as dead as they would be, assuming the hounds could overcome the demon. Certainly it would be a fight worth seeing, the hounds against the more-than-giant demon.

"After them!" Fosull ordered.

"Are you gone mad?" one of his warriors said. "You want us to pursue the hounds?"

"We are not their intended prey," Fosull said. "And they will lead me to my son. Move, quickly!"

The habits of obedience were strong in the Vargs, and the warriors followed their leader as he moved out onto the trail. Daylight painted bright streaks into the sky of night, changing the dark into light.

So far this venture had been costly and not to Fosull's liking. Time to take control and change that, the Varg leader thought. He managed a grin as he moved along the trail.

As he smiled, an early ray of sunshine gleamed from his wicked, pointed teeth.

NINE

The rising sun found Conan in a section of the swamp full of short, odd trees with broad, waxy leaves the length of a man's arm and as wide as two hands side by side. Already the fetid swamp seemed hot. Behind him in the distance suddenly came the cry of some *thing*, echoed in a moment by similar beastly voices. The calls were faint and unlike any he could recall, but his immediate worry was that the things—whatever they might be—were on his trail.

This could bode ill. The edge of the swamp lay some distance away yet, and the howls behind Conan grew louder and closer at a speed faster than his own.

Whatever made that noise would be upon him before too much longer, and Conan had no desire to meet this new threat while balanced on a narrow path in a desolate swamp. He needed a clear spot in which to make his defense, a place with room in which to move and use his blade to its best advantage.

The Cimmerian began to run, trusting his memory to keep him to the winding trail. As he recalled, there were places not too far ahead that offered safe footing, one in particular that might serve him. With good fortune he might arrive there in time.

Aye, with good fortune he would have never come to be in this predicament in the first place. True, he had escaped the cage, but smiling luck had played only a small part in that; to die a few hours later would hardly be much improvement. Mayhaps it was time that chance ran in his favor. Then again, Conan knew that Crom helped most those who helped themselves. The man from the frozen north would rather put his trust in a sharp blade than in the hands of the gods. A sword could be directed by skill; the gods did only as they would. A keen edge cut deeper than any prayer of which Conan had ever heard.

With the things baying distantly at his back, Conan ran.

The wagon in the small clearing off the road was a welcome sight, Dake had to admit, if only to himself. Nothing had been disturbed, and the freakmaster hurried to remove the simple spell that protected the conveyance and its grazing beasts. The scene was as he had left it, and the lack of any half-digested meals upon the short grass indicated that none had come near the wagon in his absence.

"Harness the animals," Dake ordered his crew.

As they obeyed, the mage smiled. This entire adventure had been without major impediment. He had four new additions to his menagerie, and Shadizar lay waiting. Along the route there were a number of smaller towns and villages in which he could hone his performances, and even earn a few coins, to arrive at his final destination in good fettle.

Yes, if a man had wits, he could rise to the top like the finest cream. By the time they reached Shadizar, Dake would have his presentation ready to amaze the rich merchants and thieves who ruled the city. They would vie for the right to sponsor him, he was certain of it.

He watched as Sab harnessed one of the oxen, the man's four arms moving with practiced speed and grace over the beast of burden. Was Sab alone not amazing? Who else had such a wonder on display? Indeed, who else had a collection to equal a four-armed man, a catwoman, a wolfman, three giants, and a green dwarf? No one, Dake answered himself.

The oxen were finally in place, the wagon ready to depart. Dake considered the logistical problem of Teyle for a moment. Although the interior of the wagon would carry a dozen normal-sized men in tight if relative comfort, the vehicle had not been designed with one such as the giant woman in mind. True, space could be made for her to lie easily, and she could sit, did she do so resting upon the floor, but moving around inside would be a problem for her. The interior roof barely cleared Dake's own head when he stood, and a rough road would sometimes bounce him enough so that he struck the ceiling when he was standing. Teyle would have to crawl in order to move about inside, and while that might be an interesting and pleasant sight to behold, it might also rub raw spots upon her knees.

Dake wanted to avoided marring her if at all possible. This was not due to any weak-willed worry on his part; he would butcher any or all of his thralls if absolutely need be, but there was no point in damaging valuable goods unless one had no other choice. No, better she should ride out front with Penz. The driver's platform had an overhanging roof to keep rain and snow off, and was high enough to that even Teyle could sit there without bumping her head. She could crawl inside to sleep when necessary.

Having solved that small worry, Dake ordered his crew into the wagon, save for Teyle and Penz. As the massive cart rolled from its concealment toward the road, Dake stood on the rear step, holding on to the door's frame, and looked back toward the unseen village of the Jatte. He marked it well in his memory. Should anything happen to the three giants he had collected, he could always return for more.

He smiled as the wagon achieved the road. Fame and fortune awaited ahead, and not more than an easy journey lay between them and himself.

* * *

Raseri, along with three of his best hunters, moved along the path through the swamp, following the hellhounds. They had come to the bigleaf trees, and the tracking beasts were far ahead, so far that only an occasional faint howl reached the Jatte's ears.

The leader of the giants was not one to trust either the gods or fortune, believing that examination and documentation served the Jatte better than wishes or prayers. While most of the experimental material gathered about the barbarian his daughter had captured had been destroyed in the fire, not all of it had been lost. Raseri had taken samples of the small man's hair, his clothing, even a patch from the sheath of Conan's sword, to compare against samples taken from others who had occupied the cage. These items had been kept in the root house, in the deepest and coolest corner where sometimes frost formed even on the hottest summer days. The Jatte had long ago discovered that cold would preserve once-living things considerably longer than open exposure allowed.

It was the faint scent of these samples that the hellhounds followed, and they would continue to seek that odor until they found the escapee. Raseri had known the beasts to follow a trail five days cold; there was no animal in the swamps able to overcome a pack of hellhounds. If Conan had blundered into a patch of quicksand and drowned, the hounds would recover the corpse. If some greatcat had eaten the man, the hounds would bring that back. Even if no more than a few patches of the barbarian remained, they would be enough to draw the hounds.

Raseri moved along the trail at a steady pace, in no great hurry. There was no way they could manage the speed of the hounds, just as there was no way Conan could outrun them. Like as not, the four Jatte would be met by the tracking animals returning home with whatever bits of barbarian gristle and bone remained after they had savaged him.

The leader of the Jatte did worry about his missing three children, though. How a single man could abduct a trio, the smallest of whom were his own size, was a mystery to Raseri. One that he looked forward to solving. Soon.

Ahead of the leader, Lawi, the youngest of the four Jatte on the hounds' trail, called out. "The left turning," he said.

Raseri nodded and waved at the other two Jatte behind him. These were the brothers Kouri the Older and Hmuo the Younger, and also Raseri's nephews once removed. "To the left."

The four Jatte took the left tine of the trail's fork, following the distinctive tracks of the hell-hounds.

From far ahead came the barely discernible yowls of the hunting beasts. Closing in on their prey, Raseri hoped.

Conan found the clearing he recalled. It was to the left of the trail, bounded on one side by a loop of stagnant pond covered with virid scum and darker green lily pads. A semicircle of swollen-based trees grew thick upon a slope that dropped sharply away, directly opposite the trail. On the side to the immediate right grew smaller trees and an underbrush of thorny brambles. Save for the trail's opening, not much wider than Conan's arm span, there was no easy entrance to the clearing.

Unless his pursuers could walk on water or bull their way through the wicked thorns at speed, they would have to come into the clearing in a single file, which, Conan felt, gave him an advantage. The beasts could circle around and come up the slope, assuming they were smart enough to recognize that option; even so, they would be slowed greatly by such a maneuver. Could they swim, they could cross the pond, but again at a reduced speed. He did not know how many of the things trailed him, nor did he have any idea as to their size or capabilities, but there was little choice in the matter. The sounds of the approaching pursuers grew closer, and if volume was any indication, they were nearly upon him.

Conan moved into the clearing, halting just inside the entrance, and unsheathed his sword. He stood with his back against the underbrush, hidden from a viewer upon the trail. He took several deep breaths, gripped the sword's handle in both hands, and lifted the blade over his right shoulder as might a man about to split firewood with an axe. He was as ready as it was possible to be, he decided. He managed a tight grin. Were it his time to die, he would do so with his sword in hand and he would go down swinging iron death at his killers. A man could do much worse, and no man would live forever.

Ho, Crom, he thought. Is today my day to join you?

The God of the Mountain did not deign to reply. Just as well, Conan thought. He would rather not know that answer until it came.

Fosull and his warriors moved along the empty trail, dodging a patch of quicksand and skirting a pond that had grown to nearly reach the path, listening to the Jatte's hellhounds howling ahead of them. The leader of the Vargs had already thanked several favorite gods for sparing him and his from the beasts, but that mercy did nothing to return Vilken or to avenge the deaths dealt by the out-swamp men. Given the nature of the hounds, it seemed likely that those unfortunate men would be torn to bloody tatters long before the Vargs arrived upon the scene. Too bad, since Fosull would have liked to deal the offenders pain and suffering on his own; still, dead was dead, and if the gods chose to use the hellhounds as their agents, Fosull was not one to argue with them. Could they recover his son, he would be satisfied. A few scraps of meat for the pot would certainly not be looked upon askance, should that favor be also granted, but not at the cost of facing hellhounds or monstrous demons.

Nay, he and his would be content with what bounty the gods elected to allow them, Fosull decided.

The rear scout came running up, all breathless.

"Yes?"

"—J-J-Jatte, my leader." He had to pause for air.

"Where?"

"Behind us."

"How many? How far?"

The scout held up one hand with the thumb folded into his palm. "F-four. Maybe an hour back."

Fosull considered this information. He had, he saw, fourteen warriors. In a confrontation with four Jatte, he might prevail, though he would like better odds. Still, were they an hour back, a fight might be avoided. If the hounds brought the out-swamp men to earth, it was possible that he and his troops could retrieve Vilken and disappear into the swamp, using small animal trails the Jatte would not chance. It seemed a workable plan, and at the very least, the Jatte would not happen upon them in less than an hour.

"Quicken your pace," Fosull called to his warriors.

The fifteen Vargs hurried along the trail.

Conan could now hear the footfalls of the approaching pursuers, so close were they. He took another deep breath, released half the air, and held the rest. The sword was rock-steady over his shoulder.

So fast did the thing enter the clearing that Conan's cut took it above the hindquarters instead of in the neck. The shock of the strike vibrated up the Cimmerian's hands and was absorbed by his thickly muscled arms. The blued-iron blade sheared through the animal's backbone and was very nearly wrenched from Conan's grip as the beast howled and went limp. Conan clung to the handle with all his might, and the wounded creature fell away from the sword and skidded to a stop two spans away. It quivered and tried to move, but only the forepaws still worked.

Ugly brute, Conan had time to see. Bigger than a big dog and not like anything he had ever known before. He moved to the half-paralyzed beast and cut at it again, this time connecting with the back of the neck and nearly severing its head. The thing quivered a final time and died.

More of them were coming, lagging behind the leader, and the Cimmerian readied himself for the fight. He stepped out into the path, sword held ready to slash.

The second beast bounded into view, spied Conan, and hurtled itself toward the man. Conan allowed the thing to get within range, then swung the heavy blade from right to left; at the same time he jumped to his right, so that the end of the sword chopped into the side of the animal's head. The strike was fatal, for the—for what of a better name—dog tripped and rolled past Conan and did not move.

The third dog to arrive scrabbled to a halt at the entrance to the clearing and sniffed the air repeatedly as Conan stepped into view again, sword pointed at the next enemy.

Likely the thing smelled the blood of its companions, Conan judged, for this one held its position and made a whining noise.

After a moment, three other of the hellish dogs arrived to stand next to this one. These too sniffed at the air, and all of them milled about for a moment as if confused.

"Ho, dogs! Come in and die!"

One of the remaining four leaped forward, and the other three followed it.

Conan sprang to meet the charge, and his movement must have startled the attackers, for the leader stopped abruptly and the three behind it slammed into it. One of those in the rear fell into the pond, gave a catlike yowl, and started to scramble out.

Taking advantage of the confusion and the fact that the dogs had to come at him one after another, Conan charged.

The leader tried to turn but could not manage it for the others blocking its retreat, and Conan's blade opened the dog's side from shoulder to belly. Crimson gouted, and the dog bit at the moving blade, but far too slowly.

Conan drew back the sword and thrust it point first. The blade entered between two ribs at a spot where he judged the thing's heart would be. The dog howled and leaped up, knocking its nearest comrade into the nest of thorns opposite the scummy pond. The wounded dog leaped at Conan but fell short as the man hurriedly backed away; then the dog collapsed, blocking the trail.

One dog, upon the path, was moving backward. Another was trying to dig itself from the tangle of brambles and only becoming more enmeshed, and the third beast, the one in the pond, was about to regain the narrow trail.

Conan took three quick steps, put his foot upon the back of the dead dog on the trail, and leaped at the one behind it.

The dog turned and ran.

Even as he came down, Conan hacked at the dog in the pond. The thing lifted one fat paw, as if to ward off the strike, and then the sharped iron sliced the leg through.

The beast howled and fell back into the water. It tried to swim but the missing leg off-balanced it, and it began to move around in a tight circle.

The brambles still held one animal prisoner, and Conan turned to deal with that one.

But as the Cimmerian moved to dispatch the struggling beast impaled upon the hundreds of thorns, the dog that had retreated along the trail must have regained its courage, for it returned and leaped, its dripping fangs aimed at Conan's throat. As he twisted to meet the threat, Conan slipped upon a patch of blood on the trail and fell to one knee. The accidental move saved him, for the attacker flew over the man's suddenly lowered form and landed upon the dog still trapped in the thorn bushes, the weight driving them both deeper into the brambles.

The swimming dog had nearly completed another circle and was facing the trail when Conan pierced its neck with his sword's tip. The greenish water turned ruby as blood pumped from the dog. It continued to struggle, but to no avail. Even as Conan turned away to deal with the two still wrapped in their blanket of thorns, the dog in the water sank.

One of the final two dogs scrambled free of the plants that held it, only to meet bloody iron.

The last of the monster dogs reached for Conan with fangs smeared with its own blood, but it could not move freely with its rear still held fast by the myriad small hooks dug into it, and the man's blade sang its song of death once more.

After Conan's heart slowed and he wiped sweat and gore from his face, he looked around at the carnage. Six of the things, all dead. He felt suddenly tired from his exertions. It was often that way after a battle, but there was no time to rest. He had triumphed over these formidable beasts, but their masters must surely be not far behind. Dogs, even such as these, were one thing. Giants were another.

He wiped his blade clean on the fur of one of the dead dogs, resheathed the sword, and made his way back to the trail. He turned away from the Jatte village and took up his route. At the very least, he had provided the Jatte with some measure of his worth and repaid them somewhat for his stay in their cage of torture. He would have had it be Raseri who lay slaughtered here, but the leader of the giants would find a surprise when he came for his dogs.

Conan smiled at the thought.

TEN

When Fosull's forward scout came running back, he bore news that sounded unbelievable.

"My leader! The hellhounds! They are dead!"

"All of them?"

"All of them."

Fosull considered that, but spoke to it no further. He would not have his warriors see him disturbed, even by such news as this.

The band of Vargs continued on to the site where the fight had taken place. They were dead, all right. Half a dozen of the most vicious animals in the swamp, cut down by what appeared to be a sword. Incredible.

Fosull inspected the area, observed the tracks, and like any Varg with only one eye and less than half a brain, quickly came to realize that the hellhounds had been slain by a single man. One of the outswamp ones, and likely the same half-naked man who had killed several of his warriors at the outskirts of the Jatte village. There were no prints or signs of the group that had fielded the demon.

This was bad. Very bad. Six hounds killed by one man. Here was a warrior to avoid, unless he was on your side, and he and his troops were following him instead of those who had taken Fosull's son. Not a good idea.

His warriors looked at Fosull expectantly. Despite his awe, he was the leader and it fell to him to present an appearance of non-concern, if not of outright nonchalance.

"I had thought there were more hounds," he said.

The scout, a fleet-of-foot young Varg of nineteen seasons named Olir, blinked and stared at Fosull. "My leader?"

"I thought there were eight or nine. To slay that many would have been a fair chore. But a mere six ..." He allowed his words to trail off as he tested the obsidian tip of his spear with one callused thumb. The implication was that he, Fosull, could have taken six hellhounds without raising a decent sweat.

There was a murmur among his warriors. Disbelief, Fosull reckoned, but he smiled anyway. One did not get to be—and remain—leader without a certain prowess, and it had been a dozen seasons since anybody had challenged him at anything. The last to try him had eaten Fosull's spear before he could do more than stamp his feet and wave his own weapon. More than half of this band had been but children when Fosull had slain that challenger, and the story had been embellished over the seasons so that many of the younger warriors thought Fosull invincible. Even so, somebody who could slaughter six hellhounds and walk away was no one with whom they wished to trifle.

"We waste our time here," the leader of the Vargs said.

"We are going to follow the one who did this?" Olir asked.

"Of course. I expect that he shall lead us to the others. Vilken remains their captive, or had you forgotten?"

"N-no, my leader."

"Then let us depart. Go and scout, and see that you don't trip over our quarry."

Fosull watched Olir as he moved off ahead of the others. His pace was slower than normal, to be sure. And Fosull was more than a little certain that the young Varg would do everything in his power to avoid happening upon the man who had slain the hounds. As would Fosull, were he the scout.

Lawi was pale as he returned to the spot where Raseri and the other two Jatte sat finishing their hastily packed midday meal. The group rested in a small hollow formed by the larger branches of a lightning-felled tree. Moss coated much of the downed timber, whose wooden body had lain here for at least five seasons.

"Have you determined why the hounds have

gone silent? Have they caught up with their prey already?"

Lawi shook his head and sat down upon a fat log that angled up from the mire on the side of the trail. "Aye, they caught up with the one we seek."

"That is good—" Raseri began.

"Nay," Lawi cut in. "The hellhounds are dead."

"What? Impossible!" That from Kouri.

"It cannot be!" Hmuo said.

Raseri withheld comment.

"Come and see for yourselves."

When the four giants arrived at the scene of the slaughter, it was Kouri who spoke first: "Varg tracks! So that is why the hounds are dead. A large party of Vargs were here!"

Raseri bent over one of the dead hounds, then moved to examine a second, and then a third. "Nay," he said. "These wounds were not made by Varg spears."

"Then who—?" Hmuo began.

"Conan of our cage. See?" He pointed at a gaping wound. "This was done by a sword. Examine the other three and you will find like injuries."

"You say that all six were killed by *one* small man?"

Raseri turned toward Kouri. "Aye. He is most resourceful, as we know by his escape from the cage and his flight along the trail. And never have we captured a fiercer example of the small men. You should recall that."

Kouri raised one hand to his forehead and rubbed at it. When the caged Conan had been attacked by the four Jatte with staves, it had been

Kouri who had lost his weapon to the small man and been slammed unconscious for his trouble. It was unlikely that Kouri would forget that episode.

"But what were the Vargs doing here?" Lawi asked.

Raseri shrugged. "Who can say? Perhaps they wished only to obtain a meal."

"But they continue to follow the man after seeing this. Surely even the Vargs cannot be that stupid?"

Raseri mused upon this for a moment. "It is odd," he finally allowed. "And most interesting. They must have compelling reasons. We have seen the same thing and yet we also continue to follow, is this not so?"

Hmuo said, "Regarding that. I have examined the trail carefully and have yet to see Jatte tracks. What of Teyle and Oren and Morja? It would seem that they are not with the fugitive."

That was even odder, Raseri thought. But surely there must be some connection between the barbarian and his own missing children? That Conan had escaped from the cage alone was most difficult to believe; mayhaps he had had help. It might be that he had comrades unnoticed by Teyle when she captured him. Perhaps these comrades had freed Conan and then taken the children for revenge, fleeing along another of the trails?

Raseri had to admit that the hypothesis seemed farfetched; still, one had to account for the reality somehow, and that Conan had escaped and his son and two daughters had disappeared at the same time were facts. How these things had come to pass might be difficult to ascertain, but the ways of reason dictated that for every effect there was a cause. Whatever else happened, Conan must be captured. What he knew could be determined only after that was accomplished.

Raseri nodded to himself. Aloud, he said, "Come. There are no more answers to be gained here. We must catch Conan."

"And get past the Vargs to do it," Kouri said.

"If need be, we shall do so."

Conan made good time along the trail. The swamp was thinning; there were now patches of dry land that extended for long stretches along the path, and he knew it would not be long before he regained the road to Shadizar upon which he had met the giants.

The Cimmerian considered himself lucky to be free, and his intent was to continue his trip without further adventures into danger, could he avoid them. He was alive, albeit somewhat hungry, and with each moment that passed, he moved farther away from both giants and dwarves. He would be glad to be shut of the swamp.

Only moments later Conan found a kind of berry he recognized as edible, and he paused long enough to make a short meal of the things. 'Twas not as solid as meat or fowl, but better than listening to the rumble of his empty belly. He wiped his mouth with the back of one hand and continued on his way. He would, if his memory served him correctly, be nearing the road soon. It would not come fast enough to suit him.

* * *

The wagon rolled along the bumpy road, and Dake fell into a doze, lulled by the rocking motion. He had a dream. In the dream he was master of a huge circus, a hippodrome packed with thousands of spectators, all of them watching the hundreds of oddities that he had collected and bred. Cat-women performed acrobatic dances; four-armed men and women juggled dozens of colored balls; green dwarves and towering giants paraded back and forth; wolfmen fought each other with tooth and nail. All of this took place under the largest tent in creation, a high-peaked, blue-and-white-striped roof of pure silk that shaded the viewers in the stands.

Suddenly there was a *crack!* and one of the huge poles holding the tent aloft snapped. The billowing silk collapsed upon the throng of customers and freaks; people began yelling at Dake for help. "Dake! Dake! Dake. . . ."

He awoke to find Kreg shaking him. "Dake."

The mage slapped his assistant's hand away from his shoulder. "Why do you disturb my slumber?"

At the same moment of his question, he noticed that the wagon was not moving.

"Why are we stopped? I did not call for a halt!"

Kreg shook his head. "We have broken a wheel."

"What? Show me."

Dake alighted from the rear of the wagon and followed Kreg around to the front. The wheel on the side upon which Teyle now sat next to Penz was indeed broken. At least four of the spokes had shattered or cracked badly, and a segment of the circle under the protective iron rim was knocked loose, the rim itself flattened where the support had failed.

"By Set's scaled scrotum! What happened?"

Penz looked down from where he sat. "We rolled over a large rock that had a larger hole behind it."

"Fool! Why did you not go around it?"

"No room. See for yourself." Penz pointed back along the road, and it was apparent that what he said was true. The road had narrowed where the protruding rock jutted up from the surface, and one side was lined with brush while the other dropped sharply into the shallow ravine.

Dake cursed again, calling upon several lesser-known gods, and describing some of their more disgusting personal habits in his imprecation. The malediction was enough to make the oxen stamp their feet nervously.

Finally he said, "Unpack the spare wheel and replace the broken one."

Penz grinned, showing his wolfish teeth. "Alas, we cannot. We have already used the spare wheel. Recall the ascent of the Haraan Pass?"

Dake clenched his fists in voiceless rage. Yes. They had not had time for a wheelsmith to construct them another since the accident. And the weight of the massive wagon was such that all six wheels were necessary for support.

"Can you not use your magic to effect repairs?" Kreg asked.

No, he had no such spell, but Dake did not deem it wise to reveal the limits of his powers to anyone, much less his weak-brained assistant. "Magic is not to be wasted on such mundane chores," he said. "You and Penz and Sab shall take the wood-cutting tools and carve replacements for the broken parts. There are sufficient trees about for suitable lumber."

"But—but that will take hours!"

"So? I am disposed to enjoy the countryside for a time."

"What countryside? There is nothing here but a patch of forest and a red-dirt road."

"Hold your tongue, idiot, or lose it!"

Kreg glowered, but fell silent. He knew well that Dake had but to wave Penz on and the wolfman would delight in tearing out Kreg's throat. Or Dake could simply put his obedience spell on his assistant and have him stand fast while the freakmaster smashed Kreg's head with the nearest handy rock. Kreg had seen his master kill before, and he knew well that murder bothered Dake not one whit.

"Sab! Bring the cutting tools!" Kreg bellowed. "And get yourself down from your perch, hairy face!"

Penz leaped from the driver's seat, landing lightly, and continued to grin at Kreg. Dake saw that Kreg's insult had no effect, for the wolfman was taking great delight in Kreg's barely controlled anger. Ah, a pity, but certainly Kreg was nearing the end of his usefulness. If Penz behaved himself, perhaps he would be allowed to dispatch his tormentor to the Gray Lands.

As the trio moved to locate wood sufficiently dry and unrotted with which to replace the spokes and broken wheel segment, Dake looked for a shady spot wherein to continue his nap. Mayhaps his dream would resume itself. That would be pleasant.

ELEVEN

Once he regained the road, Conan increased his pace, enjoying the feel of the solid ground beneath his sandals. His powerful legs, made strong and sturdy by lifting heavy rocks and logs as a boy in Cimmeria and subsequent years of walking and running, propelled him along with effortless strides.

He was, he reflected, little the worse for wear. He had his sword, and the adventure with the giants had cost him some comfort and time, but little else. Shadizar and wealth lay before him, and he would not be deflected from his goal again.

As the sands of the day trickled down toward dusk, Conan found a place suitable to stay the night. He set snares, quickly caught a rabbit, and by full dark had a fire lighted and a meal cooking over it. As he tore at the roasted meat with his strong white teeth, he smiled. Someday when he was old and grizzled, he could tell the story of the giants and the green dwarves to his grandchildren. Until then he would waste no more of his time worrying about it, for the events were in the past, over with, done.

"The wheel is repaired," Kreg said. His face and hands were begrimed with dirt and axle grease, blended artfully together with sweat, and he stank in the bargain.

Overhead, the partial moon shined her pale and waxy light down upon Dake and his party.

"It has taken you long enough," Dake said. "There is a stream down the hill. Go there and clean yourself and your garments. Take Sab and Penz with you and have them do likewise, then return. It is too dark to risk travel. I do not wish to have another broken wheel."

As Kreg led the four-armed man and the wolf-man to the stream, Dake sent a glance back along the road behind the wagon. The forced stop had cut by several hours the lead they had gained on any pursuers. True, it was unlikely that followers would march through the swamp at night, and any of the giants who might have taken up the chase were likely still half a day behind, even considering the broken wheel. Be that as it might, Dake would feel better once the sun reclaimed the night and allowed them to continue their journey.

When Kreg and the others returned, he had them move the wagon from the road and into a small clearing near a grove of reddish-barked evergreen trees. As the night's chill settled over them, the unusual band climbed into the wagon and slumbered.

Fosull slept badly, tormented by dreams. His night visions were peopled by huge red demons, half-naked outswamp men, Jatte, and other shadowy figures he could not recognize. Fosull, fleet of foot and quick of arm while awake, found himself unable to run faster than a crawl in the dream, and all the power of his arm could hurl his spear but at the speed of a falling leaf. Where normally he wore his kilt of soft deerskin around his loins, he was naked. He kept trying to find his hut, but was hopelessly lost within the warrens, unable to recall the path leading home. During one frantic flight from a herd of four-armed catwomen, Fosull realized that he was dreaming; even so, he could not shake himself from the nightmare upon which he rode.

This dream was not, he managed to think, among his better ones.

Raseri lay awake long into the night, turning over possibilities in his mind, considering, thinking, trying to make the events of the past two days fit into a neat package. It was difficult, nay, more, it was not yet possible to do so. Too many variables had yet to be eliminated. Raseri could not devise a single theory that would account for what he knew.

The leader of the Jatte was sorely perplexed. Generally he could determine the reasons for happenings. Of course that might be because most of the things in his world were simple on the face of them, and easily laid to rest. Here instead was a complex problem unlike any he had dealt with before, and while it distressed him on one level, on another he found it quite invigorating. One's satisfaction at solving a difficult situation would be proportionately greater than the satisfaction of handling a simple problem.

Raseri smiled at the thought. That he would resolve the problem was a certainty; the questions were when? and where? and how difficult?

He was worried about his three missing children, of course, but he reasoned that they were in no great danger, at least for the time being. Had the abductors—and he was now sure that there were more than one—wished to kill the kidnapees, they would hardly have taken them so far away from the village to do so. No, likely the child-stealers had some other use in mind for Teyle, Oren, and Morja. Perhaps they had in mind experimenting upon them, like he had done with Conan. Or displaying them. There were many possibilities, and Raseri sorted through as many of them as he could before sleep claimed him.

Conan arose early, prodded by a desire to put more distance between himself and his nearly fatal visit with the giants. Even as the first glimmerings of dawn sparkled redly through the skies, the Cimmerian was up and walking, eating the remains of another cooked rabbit as he moved, pausing only long enough to wash down the meat with a handful of water from a brook near the road.

By the time the day was fully alight he had been on the road for the better part of an hour.

As he crested a slight rise in the highway, he saw in the distance, stopped next to the side of the road, a wagon. Quite large it was, and perched upon six wheels. Eight or ten oxen grazed near the conveyance, which was roofed and very nearly the size of a house.

Conan loosened his sword in its sheath as he stepped from the road into the cover of a stand of small trees. His recent adventure had reinforced his caution, and while the inhabitants of the large wagon might be harmless, he was not disposed to trust them sight unseen.

The big Cimmerian moved easily through the trees, taking care to do so quietly, keeping some measure of cover between himself and the wagon.

He found a spot covered with dried tree needles and squatted down behind a scraggly bush to observe the situation. He would watch for a time and see what transpired.

After a few moments a fair-haired man emerged from the vehicle, followed by another man wrapped in the folds of a robe and wearing a cowl. Conan was unable to see this second man's features clearly, but the third man to exit the wagon was another matter.

This man had no fewer than four arms.

Conan was reflecting on this oddity when the wagon creaked and shook, and a giant woman, bent to avoid hitting her head on the door frame, emerged. When she straightened, Conan saw at once that the woman was Teyle, of the Jatte.

Decidedly strange, he thought. The strangeness increased when the Jatte twins, Oren and Morja, followed their older sister. Behind them came a woman covered in short fur, with the face and features of a cat. And behind her there came a mottled green dwarf, whose kin Conan had recently met.

He continued to watch as the fair-haired man and the four-armed one collected the oxen and harnessed them to the wagon. The cowl covering the face of the second man Conan had seen fell away as he examined the front wheel of the wagon, and Conan saw then a face that reminded him of a dog. No, he corrected his thoughts, not a dog, but a wolf.

What an incredible collection of people. All gathered together under the roof of one wagon. What could it mean?

"Do you find my freaks interesting?" came a voice from behind Conan.

The Cimmerian spun and came up, drawing his sword as he moved.

"No, this will not do," the man said. He mumbled something Conan did not understand and made a casting motion with one hand.

Conan shifted quickly to one side and raised the

sword to strike. How had the man managed to come upon him without being heard? There were few who could stalk so close to him, and this rather ordinary-looking, swarthy man, with his black hair and long mustache, seemed an unlikely candidate. While he did not appear to be armed, this fact did not dispose Conan to lower his blade.

"Put that thing away," the man said. It was not a request, but an order from the tone of it, and Conan started to laugh.

The sound died in his throat as a deathly chill gripped him and he felt his arms obeying the stranger's commands. It was as if bars of lead had been laid upon his wrists, weighting them heavily, forcing his hands downward.

Conan strained against the force that held him. Sweat sprang up and beaded on his face and shoulders as he resisted the incredibly strong pull. For a moment, the sword halted, quivering in the cool morning air.

The stranger frowned.

The blade began to shake harder. Even though he resisted with all his might, the muscles of Conan's shoulders and arms bunched, the tendons standing out under his tanned skin, the point of the blued-iron sword beginning again to settle toward the mouth of its sheath.

The Cimmerian watched himself as he inserted the weapon into the scabbard, and it was as if his arms belonged to another man.

"That is much better," the dark man said, grinning.

The realization of what had just happened swept over Conan in that instant: magic! The man had put a spell upon him!

The Cimmerian laughed, hands spread to choke his captor, but the air itself seemed to thicken, so that he was suddenly pressing against a barrier he could not overcome.

"You waste your time," the man said. "I am Dake, and you will obey me, like it or not."

Conan managed half a step, the effort turning his face red with exertion.

"You are very strong," Dake observed. "Perhaps instead of merely killing you, I can find some use for you. How are you called?"

Conan, realizing the futility of trying to attack the magician, ceased his attempt. He did not plan to speak, but the same kind of power that had forced him to sheathe his blade now pulled at his voice. He clamped his mouth shut and tried to resist.

A dozen heartbeats went past.

"Conan," he heard himself say.

"Ah, well, then, Conan. Come along."

He walked past the Cimmerian toward he wagon.

Perhaps it was useless to resist, but Conan tried. Despite his efforts, he found himself turning and following the mage. He could not stay his feet; neither could he move forward to throttle the man. The spell was powerful, more so than Conan's ability to defy it. He was like a leashed dog with a choke-strap about his neck.

As they walked down the slight grade toward the conveyance, Conan realized that it was probably magic that had allowed Dake to sneak up behind him. Teyle and her twin siblings must also be under a similar spell. He wondered how many of the rest of those assembled by the wagon were held there by this magician's curse.

Well. Like as not, he would find out soon enough.

It looked as if his intention to avoid being sidetracked on his way to Shadizar had just been thwarted yet again.

When they reached the end of the swamp without having come upon the outswamp men or Vilken, Fosull felt himself impaled upon the horns of a dilemma. To travel outside of the swamp was most dangerous. The outswamp men were not a tolerant lot, as the Vargs had learned the hard way through the years. A band of his kind invited attack, and while they could defend themselves against the odd bandit or curious farmer, there were many more of the outswamp men than there were Vargs. Fosull's grandfather had led a hundred warriors from the swamps to forage during the Great Drought some forty seasons past, and had returned with only half that number alive. The philosophy of the outswamp men seemed to be that if somebody was different from them, they should kill them out of hand.

What was to be done? He did not want his warriors slaughtered. Then again, he could not hope to retain their respect did he let his son's captors escape. Fosull knew he was growing older, and that he was no longer the Varg he once was. While he was fairly certain he could best any Varg in the tribe, he was not *positive*. Allowing his son and heir to be taken without doing everything possible to retrieve him would certainly appear to be a weakness, and any sign of weakness would bring the challenges. Such was the way of the Vargs.

Curse those outswamp men to the deepest pits of hell!

Something must be done, and while reluctant to bow to the reality, Fosull knew what it must be. A troop of fifteen Vargs could not easily remain invisible outside the swamp, but a single Varg might.

Fosull turned to his warriors. "Go back to the warrens. I shall fetch Vilken on my own."

"My leader!"

"A group of us only invites curiosity and attack. Alone I can avoid detection."

"But—but the red demon!"

"I am Fosull, I do not fear Varg, outswamp men, or demons. Do as I order."

They were reluctant, but they obeyed. They muttered to each other of his bravery to attempt such a thing alone, and Fosull knew that if he survived, he would have a stockpile of respect that would last a long time. Who would challenge the Varg who ventured alone outside the swamp to contend with a demon bigger than a Jatte?

For his own part, Fosull was not thrilled with the idea, but already he had begun to conceive a plan. Vargs had a natural camouflage in the swamp; they could blend into the background easily and remain undetected by their prey. The out-swamp men came in various sizes, some not much larger than Fosull, especially the children, and there were ways to disguise what he was.

There were always ways.

TWELVE

There was a short ladder built into the rear of the wagon and Dake used this to climb onto the wooden platform that was part of the frame of the structure. The peaked canvas would not support his weight, of course, but the beam immediately next to the ladder was both thick and wide, and a careful man could sit upon this plank and watch the road behind the wagon. Often Dake would make the ascent and sit, enjoying the heat of the sun upon his face, along with the feeling of superiority that came from being high above the ground.

Dake had, he felt, much to feel superior about.

This new addition, this Conan with the large muscles, had sparked a number of thoughts. Many of the villages in which the mage piled his trade were full of unsophisticated folk. True, a four-armed man, or a woman who looked like a cat, or any of the other freaks in his entourage, always drew those who would pay to view them; still, there was only a limited amount of profit to be made from such displays in a small village. At a few coppers each, a hundred souls did not amount to all that much.

Mostly Dake had fattened his purse in such towns by using his thralls in other ways. Many men were curious as to what it would be like to lie with a catwoman, and long-hidden silver would be produced for the chance. Penz was an expert with his rope, and contests against those who fancied themselves adepts at catching things with a noose would bring in the odd wager. The green dwarf might well prove to be good enough with that short spear to best locals who thought themselves better in throwing at targets. The giant woman might challenge the lusts of some men, though he would have to be careful there about the possibility of offspring—a miniature giant would impress no one.

More than anything, however, even in the smallest backwater village they did love to gamble. And in those places where men were hard from working the land or hunting for food, they loved to gamble on a man's physical prowess. Feats of strength, wrestling matches, fights—those were the events upon which the simple folk would wager. Dake had seen fifty silver coins, and even a few gold ones, proffered as bets upon a contest between two fighters, and this in a village where the land, houses, and belongings combined did not seem worth a handful of hollow-eared coppers.

For a man who could field a contestant who was strong and agile, there was money to be had. True enough, once they reached Shadizar, the freaks themselves would be enough of an attraction so that a fighter would not be necessary. Then again, the thieves of Shadizar had even more money with which to wager, did they not? Besides, a man with a good sword arm would make an excellent guard for all the riches Dake intended to possess, especially a thrall made loyal by a magical spell.

How adept was Conan had yet to be determined. One could not judge a man's abilities by mere appearance, albeit that the barbarian certainly looked fit and fierce enough. A few tests before they reached the next village would be in order.

Dake smiled, once again pleased with himself. A clever man would always find a spot near the top of things, did he but use his brain with care.

Inside the wagon, Conan regarded his fellow captives. They were no less odd at close quarters than they had seemed at a distance. The catwoman sat next to the multi-armed man and the two spoke together in quiet tones scarcely above a whisper. The wolfman kept his cowl up and kept also to himself. The green dwarf scratched himself under his breechskin and grinned, revealing his pointed teeth. The trio of giants merely looked glum. Currently the wagon was being driven by the blond man, who seemed the only occupant not under the dark man's magical control.

Teyle, who lay stretched at great length upon a makeshift pallet, rolled up onto one elbow and regarded Conan. "You escaped from my father's cage on your own?"

"Aye."

"Most impressive." She paused for a moment, seemed to consider something, then continued. "I am glad that you did."

This surprised Conan. "Why?"

She gestured at the interior of the wagon. "I find being held captive an unpleasant experience. I had not known how it felt before."

Conan nodded, but did not speak. Aye, he thought. Having been held against his will a number of times had never lessened his distaste for it. If anything, it only worsened his feelings each time. Slavery was not a fit state for a man—or for women.

"What do you know of this man who calls himself Dake?" Conan finally asked.

"He has some magical powers," Teyle said.

"Tell me that which I do not already know."

"He is taking us to Shadizar to be exhibited as freaks of nature. He intends to breed us and bring forth more and different kinds of beings."

"He told you this?"

"No. But his lackey, the fair-haired man named Kreg, has spoken of it gloatingly. And Tro, Sab, and Penz have verified the plot."

With this, Teyle introduced the other captives to Conan. The green dwarf was named Vilken.

The Cimmerian digested this new information and considered how best to use it.

"Escape is impossible," Penz said, as if in answer to Conan's unspoken question. "The spell the mage casts is powerful. It binds us to him and prevents us from harming him or disobeying his direct command."

Conan nodded. Aye, he had struggled with all his might and had been unable to overcome the geas. Even now he tested the bonds of the magic and found them unchanged.

Penz went on. "I have been Dake's prisoner for five seasons. Tro has been held for three, Sab for nearly as long. The spell has not weakened in all that time. We cannot act against him."

"My father can," Vilken said, showing his teeth.

Conan turned to look at the dwarf, who had a gamy odor that was unpleasant. "Your father?"

"Aye. He is the leader of our tribe. He will come for me."

"You seem very sure."

"He cannot do less and remain leader."

Conan considered this.

"And *our* father will come too," Oren said. Next to the boy, his sister Morja nodded.

The Cimmerian looked at their older sister, who also nodded and confirmed their statement. "Raseri cannot allow the whereabouts of our village to be known to the outside world of small men. And he would scarcely allow three of his children to be taken without some recovery effort."

Conan said, "Green dwarves and giants will hardly have an easy time of it wandering about in places occupied by people my size."

"My father is the cleverest of all the Vargs,"

Vilken said, not without a large measure of pride in his voice.

"And *my* father is twice as clever as your father, beast," Oren said.

Vilken bared his teeth and made as if to attack the giant boy. Oren halfway rose to meet the Varg.

"Hold!" Conan commanded.

The two stopped and looked at him.

"We gain nothing by fighting among ourselves."

"Vargs are no more than vicious beasts!"

"And Jatte are no more than stupid meat!"

"Enough!"

The Varg and the Jatte boy glanced at each other with hatred again, then at Conan. It was Vilken who spoke first. "Who elected you leader, to give us orders?"

Conan's grin was full of menace, and he knotted one fist into a fleshy hammer. "I elected myself. I do not intend to spend the rest of my life held captive. Dake's spell does not prevent me from enforcing calm."

The two would-be combatants looked at Conan and apparently decided that they would rather not test his mettle. They subsided without further demonstration or speech.

"Now," Conan said, "I want to know everything about Dake and his dog Kreg."

Raseri had considered several plans for his pursuit of those who had stolen his children and had finally settled upon the one he thought most reasonable. He sent the men of his tribe back to the village and proceeded alone from the swamp and onto the road of small men. The giant's logic gave him a simple mode by which he intended to operate. He would travel at night, keeping to well-used roads, avoiding contact with the small men except to ask about his quarry. A giant would be remarkable and a topic of conversation, but not nearly as much so as a group of such beings. By the time word could spread of a giant, Raseri would have moved onward.

Night travel held its dangers of course, but there were few beasts that could stand against a Jatte armed with spear and a long obsidian knife, as Raseri was. During the day he would sleep, hidden from small men. Conan he knew by sight, and the others left distinctive tracks. Following a trail at night was difficult if not altogether impossible at times, but Raseri figured that once a direction was established, like as not his quarry would maintain it. A check now and then with one of the small men would certainly be enough to ensure that he stay on the correct path. If he would be noticed, so too would his children, who could hardly be less conspicuous than he.

Once he caught up with the abductors, he would formulate a specific plan of attack. Generally, his intent was to slay the small men and take back his children.

He found a shady spot hidden from passing eyes and settled down to make a meal of the rabbit meat and dried fruit he carried, after which he would sleep until dark.

All things considered, Raseri was happy with his plan. 'Twas not unduly complicated, and it also allowed him some options, should the need arise. He was pleased with his thoughts as he drifted into sleep.

Fosull had already spent the morning in travel, and he had discovered that the ones he sought had a conveyance. If anything, that made things easier, for following the deep track of a wagon was a lesser problem than keeping sight of footprints. The width and weight of the vehicle guaranteed that it would have to keep to the road, or hard ground at the least, and as long as the weather held dry, a Varg of Fosull's ability could follow such ruts to the end of the world.

Perhaps more interesting was the fact that the ones who had stolen his son now traveled with at least three Jatte. One adult—a woman, Fosull judged—and two children. True, the prints of these latter were the same size as those of the outswamp men, and a lesser tracker might assume them to be so; however, Fosull knew Jatte footgear as well as he knew his own bare toes, and if those two were not Jatte, he would spit on his own father's burial pit.

Whether the Jatte had come of their own accord or not was less of a certainty, but Fosull reckoned it not likely. Jatte had less use for outswamp men than did Vargs—they did not even eat the ones they caught and killed.

A bad business, this, outswamp men who could take Varg and Jatte alike.

The few times Fosull detected travelers approaching from the opposite way, he scurried from the road and hid himself until they passed.

When the Varg reached the little-known fork that led to a tiny settlement of outswamp men, he deviated from his tracking of the wagon.

Upon reaching the cluster of several houses—they could hardly lay claim to being a village—Fosull moved with great stealth, staying downwind of the local dogs until he saw what he needed.

Hanging in the hot sunshine from a line strung between two trees was an assortment of outswamp men's clothing. The Varg spotted the item he deemed necessary and crept through the shrubbery and tall grass until he was close enough to make his sprint. Up he leaped, and quickly he dashed to the line of nearly dry clothes. He snatched a cowled robe from the hemp rope and never paused a moment in his flight. One of the dogs caught his scent and set up a furious barking, but Fosull would be far away before anyone came to investigate the source of the dog's lament. If by some chance the beast pursued him, then it would be the animal's last misfortune. Hellhounds were one thing, common dogs something else.

When he deemed that he was far enough from the settlement, Fosull considered his prize. The cloth was rough and coarse homespun, a much-faded brown that was closer to tan than the dye must have been when fresh. It was but the work of a few moments to shorten the sleeves with his knife and to cut away the hem so that it would not drag upon the ground. With the garment on and the hood raised, naught but the Varg's hands and feet were readily apparent to a passerby. Fosull located a small pond and from the edge of this he scooped up some mud, which he applied to his feet and hands, darkening them to a mottled gray. The outswamp men had among them those of short stature, children, dwarves and the like, albeit none of them were apt to be green-skinned. With the clothing and the dirt caked upon his extremities, Fosull figured to pass all but a careful scrutiny, and it was his intent to avoid giving too many of the outswamp men a chance to examine him closely.

Thus disguised, Fosull returned to the main road and resumed his journey along the trail of the wagon that carried his son.

THIRTEEN

Conan awoke from a hot sleep as the wagon halted.

The overhead canvas kept most of the sun out, but the thick cloth absorbed and then passed on the heat to the extent that the interior of the vehicle was thereby made cloying; it was a sticky warmth, devoid of breezes and less than comfortable.

His efforts to free himself of the spell in which he was ensnared had proved fruitless. Even as he came up from slumber, he tested himself against the magician's power yet again, willing his legs to carry him away from the wagon.

Again his best was to no avail. He was held more firmly than if he were wrapped in thick ropes. Hemp would stretch and give, at least, and this curse felt the same as it had when first it had been laid upon him.

"Everybody out!" Kreg ordered.

The inhabitants of the wagon trooped out into the afternoon sunshine. A small wind stirred Conan's black mane as he alighted from the step, and the air was refreshing after the enclosure of the wagon. There was a small wooded patch to the left of the road, and a field of boulders on the right, most of which were inset into the dusty red ground.

The hated slaver Dake stood nearby, grinning at his captives.

"I have arranged a small entertainment for you," he said. "Our newest addition, while not the beneficiary of nature's largess as are the rest of you, is not without a certain rough charm." He smiled at Conan, who returned the expression with a cold stare. "Barbarians tend to make good fighters, and while large muscles do not always indicate great strength, I expect that Conan is not without a certain amount of power within his sinews."

Conan glanced at his companions. Penz's face was impassive. Vilken's sharp-toothed smile played over his countenance. The catwoman and the four-armed man watched Dake, a trace of worry evident on their features. The giant children merely looked on with curiosity. Teyle towered over them all, arms folded under her ample breasts.

"There," Dake said, pointing. "That rock. Go and fetch it for me, Conan."

The Cimmerian tried yet again to resist the

magic, but it was as if his legs belonged to another. He stalked toward the boulder, a misshapen stone that was as high as his knees and as wide as his shoulders. He squatted, wrapped his thick arms around the rock and clutched it tightly with both hands. Using in the main the strength of his thighs and hips, he pulled the boulder free of the dust and stood. It weighed about as much as he did, Conan judged.

The Cimmerian walked back toward Dake. Where he stood next to the magician, Kreg's eyes widened as he watched Conan approach.

"Very good," Dake said. "You may put it down."

"Where?"

"Why, anywhere you choose. It matters not."

Conan would have hurled the heavy rock at Dake, but the magician's leave about where he could put the stone did not extend to the spot upon which the slaver stood. It was not from want of trying, however, that the young Cimmerian was unable to crush his enemy. When it became apparent that he could not use the rock to smash Dake, Conan turned away from the restraint and shoved the weight at Kreg instead.

"Set's balls!" the man yelled. He scrambled back, nearly tripped, but managed to maintain his footing and avoid being flattened by the falling boulder. The heavy rock hit the ground with a *whump!* and kicked up a small cloud of dust.

"You—you barbaric *fool!* You almost hit me!"

Conan's grin was as wolfish as any of Penz's. And in fact, Penz and the other enslaved oddities smiled at Kreg's discomfort.

Even Dake's face wore a slight grin. He said, "Not a bad effort, but surely you can do more. There, that one, fetch it to me."

Conan's smile vanished as he turned and beheld his second task. The rock did not appear to be buried, but it was larger than the first, probably half again his own weight.

The Cimmerian moved to the boulder. Its shape, much like that of a lopsided mushroom, offered convenient handholds under the lip of the cap, and while it took a great deal of straining, Conan's thews were equal to the task. His steps were solid from the weight of the rock, if slow, and he managed to keep the stone from dragging the earth as he made his way back to where Dake and Kreg stood.

"Excellent! Put it down." Dake turned to look at his assistant, then back at Conan. "Right there. And take care that you do not startle Kreg here by dropping it too close to him."

Kreg glared as Conan deposited the rock.

"One more. Ah, that one."

Conan looked in the direction of Dake's pointing finger.

The boulder was taller than Conan and easily twice his weight, he figured. It was narrow only at the top, and smooth, and offered no easy grip. Conan shook his head even as his feet moved to obey Dake's command. "I cannot see a way to lift it," he said.

"But you must try."

Rage flared behind Conan's eyes, and he felt the

heat of it burn his skin. To be ordered about like a dog, it was more than he could bear!

For a brief moment Conan felt the spell holding him slacken, if only just a little. Joy surged in him, but he did not reveal his feeling. Something had affected the curse. What was it?

In that moment the full power of the geas returned and Conan reached the subject boulder. He would have to think on it later.

There was no easy way to manage this labor. The smooth rock offered no purchase, and in any event it was too large to reach around to lock his hands together. He pondered the problem for a moment, then he had an idea.

He began to push against the top of the boulder, tilting it slightly, rocking it up from where it was buried at the base. He moved to the opposite side and shoved it the other way, then returned to his original position to repeat the action yet again. The boulder, resting undisturbed for an eon, began to teeter. This would take precise timing, Conan knew, and he waited for the rock to begin to overbalance before he ran around it and put his back against it, holding it up.

The boulder now partially rested upon the ground and partially on Conan's broad back. With great care the Cimmerian leaned forward, moving slowly, so that the weight rested more and more upon him. At the same time, he bent his knees and squatted, lowering his body so that the top part of the huge stone began to pivot over the fulcrum he had provided it. He shifted again, striving for a perfect balance, bringing his arms up to the sides to cradle the immense mass upon his back and shoulders.

The boulder came free of the ground and rested entirely on Conan's back. He had misjudged the weight, he realized; it was heavier than he had thought. If he misstepped and fell, the rock would crush him against the ground.

With steady and slow steps, Conan covered the distance between himself and the slavemaster.

"Amazing," Dake said. "I did not think that you could manage it. Put it down—I would not have you injure yourself."

Conan leaned back; the boulder slid from his shoulders and thunked against the ground. It looked as if it might topple, but remained upright, if canted at an angle.

"Sab, Penz, and Kreg, to me."

The four-armed one and wolfman hurried to their master, as did his assistant.

"Lift that stone for me."

The three gathered around the tall rock, tried to find means by which to hold it, but could not.

"Tip it, as he did."

They did try. But when the stone was overbalanced, it proved too much for the trio. Despite their efforts, the rock fell, kicking up a great explosion of dust when it did so.

"Enough," Dake commanded. To Conan he said, "You are very strong. Can you wrestle?"

Grudgingly, Conan said, "Aye."

"Do you know the fist style of fighting?"

"I have some knowledge of it."

"Are you adept at either?"

"Both."

"Good, good! We will clean out every village on the way to Shadizar! With you as my champion, we shall quite probably be rich by the time we arrive in the City of Thieves!"

Conan did not speak. The prospect of being made to fight for wagers did not sit well with him. Being made to do such a thing by magic only made it worse. Then again, it was better to be considered useful as a fighter and alive than useless and dead, by any measure of which Conan knew. Living, you had a chance to escape and wreak vengeance. Dead, you faced the Gray Lands, a prospect that he knew was much worse, having visited there via magic.

Aye, he would fight if he must. But would that his opponent were Dake.

Fosull's plan was working out better than he had expected. The few outswamp men he encountered stared, or made comments to each other about his short stature, but none offered any real bother. Perhaps they could see that his spear was sharp-tipped and smooth from use; a short man with a spear is equal to a tall man without a weapon, after all. At least that was how Fosull counted it.

As the sun smiled down from his highest perch, a wagon filled with brass-bound wooden casks appeared on the road behind the Varg; it was drawn by a team of four oxen and driven by a hugely fat outswamp man whose beard and hair seemed joined into a mass of greasy red spikes extending in all directions.

As the wagon neared, Fosull stepped from the road to allow it to pass. Instead, the fat redhead, dressed in fringed leather shirt and pants as greasy as his hair, pulled the oxen to a halt.

"Ho, short one."

"Ho," Fosull called back, somewhat suspiciously. Why had he stopped?

"Are you bound for Elika?"

Fosull had no idea where Elika was, or even what it was, but it seemed like a good idea to be bound for somewhere. "Aye," he called from beneath his hood.

"Well, then, climb up and ride, for I am also traveling to that samesaid village and I would enjoy company."

The Varg considered the idea but for a moment. The tracks of the wagon he followed lay ahead, and riding would certainly be easier than walking. The obese one seemed amiable enough. Fosull scrambled up to sit on the wide plank next to the driver.

The fat man urged the oxen forward and the wagon bounced along.

"I am called Balor the Winejack, short one."

"Fosull."

"Well-met then, Fosull."

They rode along for some way, Balor making most of the conversation and apparently content to have Fosull nod now and then or utter a word of encouragement for him to continue.

"Of course there's bandits," Balor said, "and I keep my iron babe handy for 'em." He reached under the seat and produced a short-handled battle

135

axe. The weapon had seen some use and a number of years, to judge from the nicks and rust on the blade and the worn handle, but it appeared no less effective for those. Fosull gripped his spear tighter, but Balor shoved the axe back under the seat and laughed.

"Then again, the bandits is been slack hereabouts of late. I suppose you heard about the pack of 'em slaughtered a few days back along the Corinthian Road?"

No, Fosull hadn't heard. That opening provided Balor with enough material for another half hour of talk. He explained that one of the nastiest bunch of bandits for quite a ways had been killed in the hills. From what the wolves and vultures had left, the unfortunate brigands had for the most part been sword-cut, although one had a hole punched in him as big around as a man's forearm, and what do you suppose could do *that* to a fellow?

Fosull allowed as how he knew not, and that gave Balor leave to talk about the various ways he had seen men killed over the years.

Aye, the man was as long-winded as a spring deer, but Fosull would likely not be bothered by other outswamp men as long as he was in the company of one of them, and riding was faster and easier than walking. Listening to the boring stories was a small enough price to pay.

Later, however, the Varg gained another dividend when Balor brought forth one of the kegs of wine and tapped it. A man hated to drink alone, Balor said, and surely Fosull would oblige him by quaffing a few cups of this excellent vintage, would he not?

Surely Fosull would.

The ride became more and more pleasant as man and Varg drained cups of the admittedly excellent vintage wine. Amazing what the product of the grape could do to heighten one's spirits, was it not?

Indeed, Fosull said, laughing and slapping his new companion on the back.

Indeed!

Raseri's steps were not in the realm of mythology—no magic boots to carry him a day's walk at a stride—but his long legs did move him half again as fast as a walking small man. Thus far no one had spoken directly to him or otherwise slowed his pace. A confrontation with a giant bearing a spear apparently called for more effort than most of the small men wished to expend for whatever gain might be made.

No one had overtaken the leader of the Jatte from whence he had come, and those passing from the opposite direction were soon lost to view behind him. Thus it was that when Raseri arrived at a forlorn and ramshackle inn that squatted toadlike next to the road, no one had come before him with news of passing giants.

Raseri had to bend very low to enter the building; fortunately, the structure, rude though it was with oilskin flapping over open windows and lashed-beam construction, had a high-framed ceiling, so that he could stand erect.

The Jatte leader took some interest in the reaction of the few patrons within as they noticed him. Awe, fear, surprise, all these were reflected on their faces. He judged that most of the half dozen or so were locals, farmers or shepherds. Two were women, one old and cronelike, the other younger and dressed provocatively. The inn's trull, Raseri reasoned, having been taught of the small men's custom of selling certain pleasures.

"Wh-wh-what d-do ye w-want?"

Raseri looked down at the speaker, a man wearing a patch over one eye and several scars where half his beard would have otherwise grown.

"Food. And drink."

"We h-h-have mutton and ale. And w-wine."

"Those will do."

Raseri reached into his belt pouch and produced several of the copper and silver coins he had taken from various captives over the years. "Are these sufficient?"

The greedy gleam in the innlord's eye told the Jatte chief what he wanted to know before the man spoke.

"Yes. To be sure!"

"Give me as much as these are worth," Raseri said. "What I do not eat immediately I shall take with me."

"At once!"

The younger of the women moved toward Raseri. She licked her lips, which seemed to have gone dry, and her voice when she spoke was nervous. "Would ye be wantin' anything else, milord giant?"

"Of what do you speak?"

The woman gestured at herself with one hand.

Behind Raseri, two of the men drinking ale at a rough table laughed. One said, "Feki's dreaming, eh?"

The other man said, "I think not. I think she could manage it. She handles me, after all."

"Ho, ho! So could a female mouse!"

Raseri said, "I need only food. And information. A large wagon passed this way recently. How long ago?"

The woman nodded. "Aye. Yesterday, past noon. Had a strange driver, all hooded he was, and wearing gloves, even in the hot sun."

The Jatte reached into his pouch and produced several silver coins. He handed them to the woman. "For your trouble."

The woman's face lit in a bright smile. "Thank ye, milord giant!"

Raseri shrugged and turned toward the innlord, who brought forth several slabs of cold and greasy mutton and a small cask of ale. The giant collected the food and drink and put them into the sack he had slung over his shoulder. He would walk and eat.

Were he only a day behind the wagon, he could gain upon it, for oxen were slower than he. If he walked at night, likely he could close the gap even more, for the small men seldom ventured forth during the night, even on well-marked roads. But what frightened a small man did not necessarily do the same for a giant.

Yes, this gathering was frightened of a single giant, but a dozen small men with weapons would not be, and strength did not always lie in size, but sometimes in numbers.

Raseri left the building and the mutterings of those within it behind. He chewed on the cold meat as he walked, washing it down with swallows of the ale, holding the cask as might a small man holding a cup. In a way, this trip was good, despite its cause. It had been too long since he had gone out among the small men. There was always something to be learned, and knowledge, after all, was the ultimate power.

FOURTEEN

It had been some years since Dake's last visit to the hamlet of Elika, a mere half an hour's journey along a side path to the southwest. The small track was barely large enough to allow passage of the wagon, but allow it it did. The village itself nestled within a meander of the Illitese River, a broad, cold waterway fed by numerous mountain streams born largely of snowmelt high up the southern slopes of the Karpash range.

Kreg guided the creaking wagon toward the village through stands of white-barked hardwood trees that grew so thick as to form arches over parts of the road. The land here was fertile, and warm enough year-round so that grapes were the main crop, furnishing a steady supply of the fruit for local winemakers. The Elikans also caught rainbow-colored fish in the river and grew certain grains and other fruits. As small towns went, Elika had more to boast about than did many, and while not rich, neither was it particularly poor. Many stout people lived there, always a reliable indicator of how much food was to be had.

By the time the wagon managed to lumber into the town, news of its arrival had spread, and more than a score of curious villagers—men, women, and children—had gathered to watch.

As Dake emerged from the conveyance, Kreg hurried to pull forth the thick plank that normally rode under the vehicle's belly. He unfolded a set of legs attached to the plank and latched them, so that a narrow platform was created against the backdrop of the wagon's starboard side.

The freakmaster mounted the platform and turned to face the curious. He began his spiel.

"Friends, the Master of Oddities has arrived, bringing for your entertainment all manner of wonders!" Dake waved his arms, flinging them wide, then drawing his hands back in slowly, practiced grand gestures to match his booming voice.

"For a few coppers on this very evening, you can gaze upon sights never seen before by normal men! You can behold with your own eyes the green, human-flesh–eating dwarf from the jungles of far Zembabwi! Or feast your gaze upon Tro, the cat-woman! Or Penz, the man whose mother was a she-wolf—and whose father a rogue! Too, you can see Sab, the man with four arms! And from the edge of the world, past distant Khitai, I have brought you giants!"

Dake glanced at the crowd, which increased in size even as he smiled down upon them. "Friends, one of my giants is a woman of great beauty and such proportions as to make a blind man stare." He winked at the audience and was rewarded by the laughter of several men, who understood that there would be one show for all to see—and another for men willing to pay extra.

"And aside from all these wonders, unmatched in the civilized world, I bring also Conan the Cimmerian, a barbarian fighter from the frozen north, undefeated as a wrestler or boxer in over a hundred battles! Conan invites all comers, and if there is one among you who would test his mettle, he offers two gold solons to any who can best him!"

That woke them even more, Dake saw. Most men had seen naked women, and even the occasional freak of nature, but the call of a wager wafted over the crowd like the scent of a well-prepared meal. There was always some fool long on might and short of wit who would fight anybody—or anything—for money. Dake had seen men step into a roped-off ring to challenge muzzled and declawed bears or great apes, for no reason other than the thrill of battle. The local champion would certainly be produced for the call of gold.

As more and more of the villagers turned out to hear Dake, he warmed further to his task, already thinking of the night's show. A ring of torches in the darkness would give enough illumination so that the freaks could be viewed, and it would be Kreg's job to see that everyone around the arena had paid before Dake would allow the show to begin. He would do a few illusions, perhaps summoning the demon, or the fire-that-did-not-burn, maybe even the rain of toads. Then the livestock would be brought out, one at a time, and Dake would spin a fantasy about each of them. Cat-women or wolfmen were amazing by themselves of course, but by the time Dake finished creating a past for them out of whole cloth, they would be more so.

Once the general audience had had its fill, the village women would be sent away for the viewing of Tro and Teyle, should Dake decide to show them without clothing. The wagon would serve for any willing to pay the steep price asked to lie with either the catwoman or the giantess. Probably none here could afford them, but one never could be certain unless one asked. There would be many in Shadizar who would have the means.

The same enclosed ring could be used to stage the fighting match between Conan and the local challenger. That would be last, of course, because a good fight was hard to top. Then in the morning, perhaps some rope work by Penz, or maybe a target contest with Vilken. The little ogre contended that he was expert with his weapon; 'twas best to find out if it were true before reaching larger audiences.

Yes, this would be a profitable stop, if Dake were any judge of such things, and certainly he was.

"Miracles, friends! Things beyond your imagination! Tonight and tonight only! All will want to see, for to miss it will be the regret of a lifetime!"

* * *

Within the wagon, Conan listened to Dake's deep voice.

"He speaks lies," the Cimmerian said.

"Of course he does."

Conan looked at Penz and heard the scorn in the wolfman's voice.

"My mother was no more wolf than his. She was the daughter of a nobleman in Argos. She was ravished by her own brother, thus making my father also my uncle. He was a rogue, true enough, but my condition has aught to do with true wolves."

Tro spoke, something she had seldom done in Conan's presence. "Aye, we are all of us freaks, but nothing unnatural. We are nature's errors, sports."

Teyle said, "Nay, my ancestors were magically created. But 'twas so long ago that none of us living has had any experience of it."

Sab said, "Mayhaps, but I have seen those of your size born of women smaller than I and fathered by normal-sized men. While all life might be said to be magic, you cannot fly as a bird or swim under the sea or descend into the pits of Gehenna as would a demon."

Teyle nodded in agreement.

Vilken laughed. "No, but could my people catch her, she could descend into the great cooking pit and become what the gods intended—food for the Vargs!"

At that, Oren reached over and clouted Vilken. The boy's hand was open and the blow only connected with the Varg's shoulder, but it was enough to tumble the green dwarf from the bolted-to-the-floor stool upon which he sat and send him sprawling. Instantly Vilken sprang to his feet and lunged for his spear.

Conan was faster, and he snatched the weapon away. "Hold!" he said.

"I will kill this meat animal!"

"You will sit down or regret that you did not."

Conan could see the rage boiling in the little man, and a quick glance at the giant boy showed that his fists were clenched and that his rage was a match for Vilken's.

"Let the little tree frog try it!" Oren said. "I will make him *eat* that sharp stick he carries!"

"You will also sit," Conan said. His voice was low, but stern. "Or I will spank you like you deserve."

"I am as large as you!"

"And your size means nothing. Sit."

The boy's anger bubbled, and Conan saw that he was gathering to spring, either at Vilken or at Conan himself. The Cimmerian shifted his weight slightly and prepared to stop Oren's rush—

"Do as Conan says," Teyle said.

"But—but sister, you heard this green animal insult us!"

"Another time and place, Vilken would be a threat. Here and now, it is Dake who is the enemy of all of us. Would you spend your life in this wagon? Forced to lie with your sisters to beget twisted children who will also be raised as slaves?"

Oren's anger left him as air leaves a dying man,

and he sat back upon the edge of the bed once again.

Teyle looked at Vilken. "And you, Varg? Do you plan to end your days capering for the small men at the orders of one such as Dake?"

Vilken also deflated somewhat. He shook his head. "My father will come."

"Perhaps. In the meantime, who are your allies?"

Vilken sighed. After what seemed a long moment, he returned to his seat.

Conan was impressed by Teyle's speech. That he could have defeated the giant boy and Varg, alone or together, he doubted not, but the giant woman had calmed them without lifting any more than her voice. The power of words had called forth their doubts and stolen their rage. He saw her look at him, and he nodded once, a short motion, to acknowledge her action. Conan was always willing to give another credit where it was due, especially when the deed was done in a manner in which he himself would not have behaved.

Teyle smiled at him, a thin smile but there, and returned his nod.

Well. The immediate problem was over, but what would the remainder of the day bring?

Conan found out the answer to his question as the hours wore down. Dake put the troop to work, clearing a large circle of dirt a few minutes' walk from the center of the village, surrounding it with tall torches staked into the ground. Kreg kept the curious locals away.

As the shadows of night began to paint the land, the arena was finished and the enthralled group was ordered to the river to bathe. Dake's offhand command to strip did not bother Conan, but he could see that Tro and Teyle were embarrassed by their nudity. Neither had reason to be, for while Tro was covered by a fine layer of furlike hair and Teyle was of huge stature, both were built as attractively as any woman Conan had ever known, firm of hip and thigh, and nary a wrinkle or sag anywhere. He was a young man, and of course he looked at the women. It was fortunate that the water was so cold, for it kept his attraction and interest from becoming apparent.

Clean and somewhat refreshed, the group dressed and returned to the wagon. They dined on cold meat and fruit—some kind of apple, Conan reckoned—and drank a mild, pale wine that Kreg had procured from the villagers.

Conan refrained from filling his belly, eating only small amounts and sipping lightly at the wine. A full belly detracted from a man's fighting prowess, he had learned, and too much wine sometimes produced a reckless bravery but never added more skill.

From without the wagon the murmur of the gathering villagers reached them. Quite a large crowd, Conan judged from the sounds.

After a time Dake began to expound from his platform. He spoke of far places, incredible tribes, and man and animal perversions. His voice rose and fell, now booming, now hushed, and the crowd was mostly silent, laughing at the occasional jest.

"—and from the heavens, behold!"

The villagers yelled and laughed and made a great commotion.

Small objects plopped against the canvas roof, causing the material to sag and sounding like clumps of mud when they struck.

"I thought this was an illusion," Conan said.

"An illusion with some substance," Penz said. "They look and feel real but do not last for more than a few moments before disappearing."

Dake's voice boomed again. "Like toads not? Observe! As I make them come, I send them away!"

More startled chatter from the crowd.

Kreg stuck his head into the wagon. "You are first tonight, Tro. Then Penz, Sab, Conan, Vilken, and the giants. Do not be tardy!"

As Conan was paying attention to Kreg, he did not hear some of what Dake said, but the ending was: "—and now, friends, I give you the beautiful and incredible Tro, the woman who is also a cat!"

Tro moved through the curtained doorway, and there were yet more gasps and exclamations from the audience.

Each went in their turn—Penz, Sab, and then Conan. Were he not being held in magical thrall, Conan would have laughed at the lies pouring forth from the mage's mouth. How he, Conan, had been undefeated in a hundred fights against men, beasts, and even demons. True, the Cimmerian had encountered all of those at one time or another. Some he had fought with sword, some with his bare hands, and he had won more than his share of such encounters, but Dake's stories were beyond the accomplishments of any but a god. The man made it sound as if Conan could defeat an army with the one hand while drinking a tankard of ale with the other, never raising a hair or a bead of sweat.

Vilken was produced with a similar story, and he flashed his pointed teeth as if it were all true and he was enjoying the retelling of it immensely.

Finally the three giants were brought forth, and they apparently impressed the crowd most of all, especially Teyle. Conan saw a number of men looking wide-eyed and open-mouthed at the giant woman, and he did not have to be particularly adept to understand their thoughts.

In due course the women of the village drifted away, along with a number of the men, some of whom did not seem overly willing to leave but whose wives, with tugs or shoves, prodded them to do so. When the crowd had thinned to an audience of men only and Kreg had collected more coins from each, Dake ordered Tro and then Teyle to remove their clothing and parade around naked in front of the leering assemblage.

Conan was offended greatly by this. Seeing the two uncovered while bathing was one thing; after all, all of them were slaves and he also had been forced to strip. Pandering to the lusts of these idiot villagers in such a manner, for money, angered the Cimmerian. It was not as if the catwoman and the giantess were trulls who did it willingly. They were unable to resist, and it was Dake whose purse was fattened.

After hearing the ribald comments for what he

apparently deemed long enough, Dake had the women dress and stand aside.

"Now, we have amused ourselves. Is there no man among you who will dare to face the unbeaten barbarian?" He gestured at Conan, whose glower was not faked in the least.

The men laughed and mumbled, and a name reached Conan's ears: Deri.

The crowd parted, and a man lumbered into view.

Big he was, larger even than Conan, and shaggy looking. His nose had been broken at least once and skewed to one side, and there were scars crisscrossing his chin and one cheek. Part of an earlobe was missing. He wore a leather vest, with no sleeves or shirt under it, and thick hair sprouted all over the visible parts of him. His beard and hair, both long, were a greasy brown, and the hair on his chest was nearly as dense as Penz's. Beneath a large belly was a pair of ragged wool pants tied with a cloth sash. Deri's feet were bare and nearly black with dirt, and sprouted more hair so that they looked almost like fuzzy boots, save where they were relieved by the tips of his bare toes. The toenails were long and ragged and clogged with dirt.

From the mass of his shoulders and arms, Conan guessed that Deri had done more than a bit of heavy lifting. There was a layer of fat over them, but plenty of muscle under that.

When he smiled, Deri revealed a gap where his two upper front teeth should have been.

"Aye, I dare your champion. 'E looks too pretty to be a fighter! 'E looks more like a woman!"

The villagers erupted into laughter at this lame joke.

"Are you a wrestler or a boxer, friend Deri?" Dake asked.

"Catch as catch can," Deri said. "No holds barred."

"Done!" Dake said. "Two gold solons to the winner." The freakmaster produced two coins from his belt and held them up between his thumb and forefinger. The torchlight glittered on the gold.

"Might as well give 'em to me now, I says." Deri turned and grinned at his companions. One slapped him on the back and others voiced agreement.

"We shall see," Dake said. "Perhaps some of you other worthy men would be willing to wager on the contest? So confident am I of my man that I am willing to offer, oh, say, two coins to one?"

That brought a surge of men toward Dake, waving all manner of coinage. Conan saw much copper, less silver, but even a few small bits of gold flashing in the firelight.

"Easy, friends, easy. My man Kreg shall accept your wagers. Select one from among you to hold all monies."

The serious business of betting continued for some time. During this period Dake pulled Conan aside. As the Cimmerian stripped to his loin cover, Dake said, "Do not defeat him too quickly. Allow him to throw you a time or two and we shall offer three-to-one odds and collect the remainder of their money."

Conan studied Deri as the challenger shucked his clothing. "He is not an inconsiderable opponent," the Cimmerian offered dryly.

"No matter."

"It is not you who are facing him."

"I have every confidence in you, Conan." Dake slapped one of Conan's solid and hard shoulders. "You see, Deri is fighting for money. If he loses, he shall be but as poor as he was before. But if you lose, I shall force you to stand still while I allow Kreg to use you for sword practice."

FIFTEEN

Balor was a man not at all averse to being a walking example of some of the more extreme effects of his product. At the moment the fat man lay semiconscious in the rear of the wagon, draped in what would seem a most uncomfortable manner amid the wine casks. He showed no apparent unease, however, and the only sign that he was awake took place whenever the wagon would hit a particularly deep rut or bump, jolting it. At such occurrences, Balor would usually yell, in a voice that should certainly scare small children and dogs, "Curse all the daughters of Ophir, and all of their mothers too!"

Fosull, feeling no pain or any sensations whatsoever save a warm muzziness, grinned from within the cover of his hood and shook his head when Balor once again uttered his favorite imprecation. The winejack must have had some unpleasant experiences with the women of Ophir, wherever that was.

The Varg was content to drive the wagon. They had passed an inn some hours back, but slowed only a little. A stream that looped close to the road had provided the oxen with water to slake their thirst and a bit of fresh mud to cover the patches of green that had begun to peek from under the dried dirt on Fosull's hands and face. Balor, drunk as a fly in a sun-rotted mango, had never noticed the stop.

Fosull had no idea how far ahead the village of Elika might be. He had managed to ascertain that this was a small settlement a short trek from the main road before Balor had surrendered to the gods of wine.

It did not really matter. The wagon tracks continued onward and Fosull would follow them until he caught the son-stealers. If they missed the turn to Elika, too bad. If Balor sobered in time, he could point the way; otherwise, the leader of the Vargs intended to keep to his goal.

As evening covered her face with shades of night, a damp wind began to blow, and in the breeze Fosull caught the scent of approaching rain.

Even as he sniffed the air, a faint flash of white lit the night behind them. Moments later a low grumble rolled over the moving wagon. Lightning and its slower brother thunder, Fosull knew. The storm followed them, and doubtless it would prove faster than the plodding oxen.

This was bad news. The oxen might be unhappy about the storm; Fosull was no herdsman to know about beasts of burden. Better they should be secured somewhere before the full brunt of the rain arrived. And while Vargs were hardly ants to be washed away by the odd storm, the mud with which he had only just daubed himself would certainly do so. He and the drunk Balor could always shelter under the wagon once the animals were tethered, but a cave or house, or even a thick growth of trees or bushes, would be welcome.

There was a method to gauge the distance of a storm, taught to Fosull by his grandfather. It involved counting, a skill at which no Varg was particularly adept, but Fosull could reach the number of fingers and toes that he had. When a bolt of lightning was seen, one started to count. Could one get all the way to the last toe, going slowly, the storm was at least ten minutes from arriving. Fosull had no idea of why this was true, but it worked more often than not. The reach to fewer toes or fingers meant that the rain would be closer. He would continue to look for shelter until he judged the storm to be ten minutes behind them, at which time he would secure the oxen and awaken Balor so that they might move under the wagon. Assuming he did not find better protection from the storm, of course.

What bothered Fosull more than the immediate threat of being drenched, however, was what the storm might do to the tracks of the wagon he followed. A hard storm would churn the earth into muck, and the wagon's imprint might well be lost.

Ah, well. He would have to slay that dog when it appeared, he supposed. Vargs had no control of the weather, despite the appeasement deasils the shaman would sometimes offer to the sun and gods.

The smell of rain grew stronger.

The herald rain found Raseri nearing a thin patch of young trees, far from other shelter. He knew as well as any Jatte the ways of weather, and in a village of farmers and hunters, such knowledge was considerable. The storm's brunt approaching was nearly upon him, and he expected that it would be short, but fierce.

Raseri used his obsidian knife to cut branches for a lean-to he quickly constructed against a medium-sized tree on the edge of a grove. He placed the makeshift structure well away from the larger and higher trees. It was known that the gods would sometimes hurl lightning at the tallest objects in an area, perhaps to teach them humility. The leader of the Jatte had no desire to be roasted by the gods' lightning; he had seen one of his kind so struck and the sight had not been pleasant.

It was but the work of a few minutes to build the slanted shelter and pile the lashed branches thick with the roughly woven thatch. It would hardly be proof against the heaviest-driven gusts of rain, but it would keep the most part of the water from within. Being perhaps a little damp was considerably better than being drenched and chilled to the bone.

The lean-to finished, Raseri crawled into it on

his hands and knees just as the first fat drops began to spatter around him. Lightning shattered the dark and thunder smote at his ears, but the gods chose to spare him. A nearby tree exploded and the sharp smell of boiled sap and wood filled the air for an instant even as the now-pounding rain sought to wash the stink away.

Not a fit night to be without, Raseri decided. Lucky he was to have even this much protection from it.

The villagers of Elika gathered almost to a man around the area of Dake's wagon, waiting for the fight. Bad weather was coming to add to the night's tension. Conan was aware of the rain's less-than-stealthy approach, heralded as it was by the lightning, thunder, and hard winds. The storm, however, was hardly uppermost in his mind as he circled to his left, watching carefully the man circling opposite him. Torchlight cast wavering shadows every which way, and even the dimness was not kind to his opponent.

The Cimmerian, having fought more than a few men, had thought to tie his hair back with a short leather thong, to deny Deri any easy grasp. The large villager looked to be powerful, but slow, though Conan did not count upon this latter aspect greatly. Often bigger men moved considerably faster than it would seem at first glance.

Deri feinted a grab at Conan's right wrist and followed the fake attack with a round kick at the Cimmerian's head.

Conan ducked, jumped in, and shoved at Deri's shoulder, using both hands.

The bigger man began a fall, then turned it into a dive away from the shove. He rolled into a ball and came up, spinning to face Conan.

He *was* faster than he looked, and he had some skill in tumbling. Conan added that to his store of knowledge.

Deri grinned. "Is that your best, girl-face? Mosquitoes bother me more!"

He was a talker. Some men liked to talk when they fought. Conan himself preferred to save his energy for the battle rather than to waste it in words, except when he saw some advantage in taunts. Sometimes a word could anger an opponent into doing something foolish.

" 'Twas not I rolling around in the dirt," Conan ventured.

Deri laughed, showing the large gap in his teeth. "A man needs to loosen up, don't he?"

Conan circled back to his right. A childish taunt would not reach through the thickness of this one's skull.

Deri shifted his weight, as if he were going to move to his right, then lunged suddenly, hands outstretched.

Conan dodged and knotted his right fist into a fleshy mallet. He hammered at Deri's ducked head, missed, and slammed the edge of his bunched hand into the man's back just below the right shoulder. It was like hitting a leather-covered tree trunk.

Deri grunted, dived into another roll, and twisted as he came up.

"My sister hits harder than that."

"A man needs to loosen up."

Deri grinned again. "I will loosen your limbs from your body, barbarian!"

Conan reasoned that since Deri was larger, and likely as strong as he himself was, it would be better to say out of his grip and continue to strike or kick him.

Deri rushed in again, seeking to grapple.

Conan sprang aslant to the charge and punched, the knuckles of his fist catching Deri over the left eye. The skin split under the blow, but the bigger man spun away and chased after Conan.

As the Cimmerian backed quickly from the attack, he heard Dake yell, "Stay in the ring! Who leaves it loses!"

Conan glanced down to see where his feet were in relation to the ring. The distraction proved costly.

Deri lunged, almost in a dive, and wrapped his arms around Conan's waist.

The Cimmerian hammered down with both fists, but the angle was bad and the force of his strikes was absorbed by Deri's thick back.

Deri raised from his crouch and lifted Conan free of the ground, then snapped backward and hurled the smaller man through the air.

Conan also knew something of tumbling. Even so, the angle of his fall was less than optimum, and he hit hard on one shoulder as he tried to tuck into a ball. He came up, then dived forward and rolled again.

The second roll caught Deri short. Expecting to

catch Conan standing, the village overbalanced and nearly lost his footing.

Lightning struck nearby, the sound of the thunder coming almost as one with the flash of white.

"Mitra!" someone yelled.

The light and noise drew some of Deri's attention. Conan dropped his left shoulder and charged, driving his powerful legs hard. He hit Deri square in the chest with his shoulder.

The villager went sprawling, and such was the force of Conan's rush that he nearly stepped on the fallen man. He was forced to leap to clear the obstacle.

By the time he landed, Deri was up again, though no longer grinning.

It began to rain then, a hard patter that quickly increased to a downpour.

Crom! The rain fell so hard that Conan had to wipe it from his eyes to see his opponent. At least it was not mixed with his own blood, as was the water flowing down Deri's face.

As Conan circled past Dake, the man whispered behind him: "Enough toying, Conan. You may finish him now. The rain is uncomfortable."

The young Cimmerian gave no sign that he had heard the mage speak. Toying? This Deri was as strong as a bull! If he should get a good grip—

The thought called to itself the deed. Deri lumbered forward. The muddy ground offered a poor support for Conan's intended sidestep. He slipped, not enough to fall, but enough to allow Deri to close. The larger man threw his arms around Conan's waist and laughed in triumph as he lifted him from the ground.

Strong as he was, Conan knew that Deri would break his spine unless he got free. The man's arms tightened and the pressure on Conan's lower back increased. Conan's fists against the man's back and shoulder were to no avail. Crom, the pain—!

Conan opened his hands and brought them together with all the power he had, striking Deri on the ears with the flats of his palms. The sound was loud to Conan's own ears; it must have been deafening to Deri.

The brute screamed, an inarticulate and high-pitched yell, and dropped Conan to clasp his hands to his wounded ears.

That was all that Conan needed. He snapped his foot up and connected with the instep against the big man's crotch.

Deri's eyes bulged as his hands left his ears to clutch at the new injury.

Conan drew back his fist and slammed the stunned man square between the eyes. The blow hurt the Cimmerian's knuckles, but it was worse for Deri. He fell backward like a tree being toppled. A great splash erupted when he hit the puddled ground. The rain beating down was not enough to rouse the fallen combatant, and it became obviously and immediately apparent that the fight was over. The only way Deri was going home this night would be if he were carried.

"Well done," Dake said.

Conan turned to face the man who enslaved him, and for a moment his rage blossomed enough so that he once again felt the lessening of the magic that gripped him. Not enough so that he could attack, but with a noticeable difference.

"Collect the wagers, Kreg," Dake said, turning his back to Conan. "I shall be in the wagon drying myself."

Dake moved away, splashing through the mud and puddles, toward the wagon.

Lightning flared and thunder hammered the ring and the suddenly weary Conan.

This, he decided, was not going to be a pleasant life.

He had to escape.

Somehow.

SIXTEEN

With the storm still beating upon the thick canvas roof of the wagon, Dake dried and then dressed himself in a clean robe. He grinned. Quite a profitable evening this had been. The show had drawn nearly everyone in the village and they had been captivated, as he had known they would be. Conan's battle with the gap-toothed fool had paid off even better. A pity about the storm, though. Dake had no intention of standing about in the rain while customers dallied with the catwoman or giantess in the wagon, so that would have to wait for a better night. Still, all in all, he could hardly complain. Most of the loose money in the village had found its way into Dake's purse, of that he was certain, and it seemed a good omen. A good beginning did not guarantee a good ending, but certainly it helped.

Dake moved to the doorway and yelled out into the rain. "Come inside, fools. I would not have you sicken because of the weather."

Obediently—how else?—his thralls moved to heed his command.

Rousing Balor from his stupor amid the wine casks had proved impossible, so Fosull left the man and crawled under the wagon. The oxen were tethered by their nose rings to large rocks and would not be going anywhere. When the storm broke, there was little shelter to be found, so the wagon would have to do.

As the rain showered down, Balor began to curse again, louder than before. There came a sodden *thump* as the man jumped—or more likely fell—from the wagon's bed and landed next to the rear wheel. He scrambled across the rapidly muddying ground and collapsed next to Fosull.

"Why did you not wake me?"

"I tried. You seemed content to slumber."

"I might have drowned!"

"But you did not."

"What of the oxen?"

"Tied securely."

"I do not suppose you bothered to bring any wine?"

"As it happens, I did."

A nearby flash of lightning lit Balor's face, revealing his grin. "Ah, for a small man, you are large of wit."

"Next to the front wheel."

The space under the wagon was not such as to allow Balor room to sit upright, but he was able to crawl well enough to reach the small wine cask. He returned to sprawl next to Fosull after a moment, the smell of fresh wine on his breath and beard.

"I fear the water may pool and flow under our shelter," Balor said.

"I have dug a trench around the wagon to prevent that."

"Ah, what a clever one you are! Have some wine?"

Fosull nodded. "Aye. Might as well."

But as he drank, Fosull was full of dark thoughts. This was no mild spring shower, 'twas a fierce rain. On the morrow the dirt road would quickly dry out, but it would be washed clean of recent tracks. Finding the wagon carrying Vilken would be made more difficult.

Why, he wondered, did the gods task him this way?

The innermost thatch of Raseri's lean-to had become soaked by the time the storm abated; still, the shelter had done no less than he had expected and had kept him virtually dry. As the lightnings and thunder grew distant and quieter, moving away with the heavier rains, he considered his options.

He could leave immediately after the rain stopped, but this did not seem wise. The road would be a sea of mud, and someone of his size and weight would negotiate such a venue with difficulty at best.

Better that he should wait until the sun had baked some of the water from the earth, say, until mid-morning. Had the wagon he followed at a distance been within the realm of the storm, surely it would have to wait at least that long before attempting travel. A heavy conveyance would sink even deeper into rain-softened ground than would a giant.

Yes, that would be the wiser choice, Raseri felt. Thus satisfied with his reasoning, the leader of the Jatte fell into a comfortable, if somewhat damp, slumber.

Conan's lower back ached, as did his ribs where they curved around toward his chest. He had fought against more skilled men, but few if any had been much stronger than Deri.

The fat lamp near his pallet upon the floor of the wagon guttered and sent a lazy tendril of smoke toward the already-stained canvas ceiling, painting a new line of black against the rain-sodden material.

Dake and Kreg were fast asleep, as were most of the others. Close to where Conan lay, however, Teyle was awake.

"Are you in pain?" she asked, her voice in a low whisper.

"Some. It is bearable." He kept his voice quiet, a match for hers.

"Where does it hurt?"

Conan pointed at his injuries.

The giant woman shifted slightly. Though she moved slowly and with care, the wagon creaked under her. She held herself still for a moment, but the sound did not appear to have roused any of the sleepers. Her motions were enough to bring her close to Conan. She sat next to where he lay on his back.

"Lie upon your belly," she said.

"Why?"

"My people have a technique for healing with their hands. Perhaps I can lessen your injuries."

Conan shrugged and rolled onto his belly.

After a moment he felt Teyle's hands on him. Her touch was soft as she slid her palms down to cover most of his lower back. After shifting them so that her hands were centered over the places where it hurt the most, she held them still.

Several moments passed, and Conan felt Teyle's hands begin to grow warmer against his bare skin. Soon it was as if her flesh were somehow heated from within; his own sinew grew hot under her touch. Not so hot as to burn him, but certainly of a degree higher than he would have thought possible from another's mere laying on of hands.

The warmth was soothing, if nothing else, and Conan relaxed under the giant woman's ministrations.

How long she kept her palms pressed against him he could not say, but it seemed a lengthy period. When she pulled her hands from his body, the ache he had felt was much abated; in fact, it was almost completely gone.

Conan sat up and faced the giant woman who

sat smiling down at him. Even seated, she was much taller than he.

"I have no more pain," he whispered. "Is this some kind of magic?"

She said, "Perhaps it is. I cannot say. I was taught the skill by my grandmother. She told me that anyone could learn it, so I think that if it is magic, it is of a natural kind." Her voice was tinged with sadness.

Conan felt a sudden urge to hug the woman, feeling somehow that she was afraid and in need of comfort, despite her size. From where he sat, his face was level with Teyle's large breasts; still, he leaned forward and put his arms around her and pulled her to him.

She did not resist, and her arms, as thick as his own, encircled his shoulders and tightened.

"I fear for what will happen to my brother and sister," she said, holding Conan in a grip stronger than any woman had ever done. "And I fear for what that evil man will do with me as well."

Pressed against those formidable breasts, Conan turned his head to the side and said, "Do not worry, Teyle. I will find a way to free us."

But as he stroked and comforted her, Conan wondered how he would manage to do what he promised.

When morning broke cloudlessly over the village, Dake stood on the seat of the wagon and surveyed the land around him. A vast stretch of mud existed where the ground was bare, and the vegetation was still sodden from the night's storm. The wagon would not get two spans before it became mired, he realized. They would have to wait some hours until the sun dried things up a bit before they could leave.

As the others awoke, Dake had Tro prepare a breakfast. He informed them of his conclusion regarding travel.

Vilken said, "But if we bog down, can you not have your demon pull us free?"

Kreg laughed. "Fool! The demon is naught but an illusion!"

"Kreg! Hold your tongue or I shall remove it!" Dake glared at his assistant. The idiot revealed things better kept secret. Though it hardly mattered to his thralls, Dake would not put it past Kreg to say the same thing in a room full of potential enemies. Kreg was definitely losing his usefulness, there could be no doubt of it. Something would have to be done about him, and in the near future.

Dake and Kreg left the wagon to examine the road leaving the village. After they had gone, Conan turned to the other captives. "I have no intention of arriving in Shadizar as a slave," he said. "We must try to escape."

"We have tried many times," Penz said. "To no avail."

"Have you all attempted escape at the same time?"

"Aye," Tro put in softly. "Even three together made no difference."

"We are now eight," the Cimmerian said. "Numbers sometimes lend strength."

The original three captives looked dubious.

"What is there to lose?"

Sab spoke to that. "Dake will become angry and punish us."

"How shall he know?"

"He always knows," Penz said. "The magic is tied directly to him."

"Then you may tell him I forced you to attempt it," Conan said.

The group filed out of the wagon, Conan leading the way. He slogged through thick mud, away from the vehicle and in the opposite direction taken by Dake and Kreg.

Not more than ten paces distant, a barrier stopped the Cimmerian's advance. There was nothing visible in the clean morning air, but all of a moment, Conan found himself pressing against what felt much like a wall of gigantic bow strings. The barrier gave under his hands but pushed back; after a struggle that advanced him another two steps, the wall shoved him hard enough that he could not maintain his footing in the mud, and he slid backward for two paces before stopping.

"Come and stand next to me and push," Conan ordered the others.

With all eight of the captives pressing against the invisible barrier, the resistance lessened and allowed for more give. The group managed six hard-won steps before they were halted. Slowly, the magical ward began to slide them toward the wagon, until they were back where first they had encountered the spell.

Conan's smoldering rage flamed into a hot blaze. He charged the barrier again, drawing his sword as he did so. Perhaps he could cut his way through it—

To his surprise and that of his companions, the Cimmerian managed to slosh over the muddy ground for a good fifteen spans, at least three times the distance he had managed with the help of the others. The sword was still lifted, but he had not used it. As he felt the springy tension of the spell start to halt him again, Conan let out a wordless growl of anger and cut at the force that sought to push him back.

The spell gave way!

Conan drove himself forward another five paces, his rage giving way to triumph. He was defeating the mage's curse!

As his anger faded, however, the invisible hand clutched him and hurled him backward. Conan was lifted from his feet and propelled through the morning sunshine, a rock tossed by a playful god. He hit the ground well past his startled companions and skidded through the mud, throwing up a shower of water and muck before sliding to a halt near the wagon.

Even as Conan stood and began to wipe the guck from his arms and legs, he puzzled over the event. He had been about to break free of the curse, he was certain of it. What had happened?

Dake returned with his dog Kreg at that moment, and the Cimmerian saw at first consternation, then relief, on the dark man's face.

"Tried to leave us, did you, Conan? Ah, can you not see that it is a waste of time and energy? Best you save your strength for the fights I shall procure for you on the road to Shadizar. My spell is unbreakable."

Conan continued to strip the ooze from his body, saying nothing.

"Still, I am the master, and attempts to defy me must be punished."

"Vent your anger upon me," Conan said. "I forced the others to try it."

Dake looked at his thralls, then back at Conan. "Yes, you would do that. Try to use brute strength to solve every problem. Very well, then. Suffer for it."

The mage turned to Kreg. "Hurt him. But do not do any damage, do you understand?"

Kreg grinned.

To Conan, Dake said, "Stand still and allow Kreg to chastise you, barbarian fool. And remember the lesson: To go against my wishes is futile."

Kreg's first slap hit Conan's face, and the Cimmerian stared at the man with contempt, unable to resist or to move away. While he knew it was unwise, he could not keep from taunting the blonde. "Is that your best, dog? A mosquito stings harder."

Conan saw the anger flood into Kreg's face, darkening his fair skin. The man drew his booted foot back to kick.

"Take care, Kreg," Dake said. His voice was

mild. "If he is too injured to fight, I shall inflict matching wounds upon you."

Kreg's anger seemed tempered by the threat and he put his foot down, withholding the intended kick. Instead, he stepped forward and punched Conan under the breastbone. The strike was powerful, and even the thick muscles there could not absorb all the force of it. Conan felt his wind go, and his knees buckled slightly. He did not fall, but it was only with great concentration that he stayed standing.

"I can cause pain without injuring you, barbarian."

Kreg's grin grew wider as he further proved that he could do just that.

SEVENTEEN

As the wagon worked its way slowly over the still-boggy ground, Conan lay on his pallet, Teyle attending to the new aches Kreg had given him. He was bruised, but the slaps and punches had injured his pride more than they had harmed his body.

As Teyle took away his pain, Penz sat nearby, fingering one of his hempen ropes, uncurling then recurling it into tight coils. Outside the covered doorway, Kreg drove the wagon, with Dake next to him, and those inside spoke in quiet tones when speak they did.

"He has done the same to us," Penz said. "Tro, Sab, and I have all felt Kreg's fists. He enjoys using them."

"So I noticed," Conan said. A twinge of hurt fled under Teyle's hot hands even as he spoke.

"It is better not to anger him," Sab added.

Conan essayed a shrug, difficult to do while lying facedown. "A man enraged often loses his control. I thought to cause him to expend more energy and thus finish sooner."

"That was brave. He could have hurt you," said Oren.

"I was consoled by the knowledge that Dake would punish him did he do so."

"A risky business," Penz said.

"All of life is a risk, friend."

"Well, at least now we know that we cannot break Dake's spell," Teyle said.

For a moment Conan considered telling his fellow prisoners what conclusion he had reached about that, but then decided against it. While he felt he could trust them, it was possible that Dake might be able to compel them to supply answers to questions they might not otherwise heed. That the freakmaster was wily and dangerous was a given. What his companions did not know, they could not reveal. Better for them. Better for him.

For the spell *could* be broken, Conan felt.

Despite his lack of civilization's manners, Conan was no slackwit when it came to reasoning. Those times when he had most successfully resisted Dake's magical enthrallment had been when his rage had been at its strongest. On each occasion, as his anger had lessened, so had the the geas reclaimed him. He had very nearly broken free when last he tried, and he reasoned that his elation at near release had dampened his anger sufficiently so that he had failed.

This was powerful knowledge. A sword was a good weapon, but knowing how to use it made it a dozen times better. Armed with this new understanding, Conan now had a plan, which he would confide to the others at the proper time. Under this plan he surmised that if they could all grow as enraged as had he, surely they could overcome the magical barrier and escape. The gods must know they had just cause.

'Twould be best to attempt it when Dake was not around, for there was nothing to prevent the mage from reinstating the curse, and furthermore, burning anger could not be maintained forever. Then again, once outside Dake's influence, a strong arm might hurl a spear or rock that would end the man's threat permanently.

It was, as these things went, a simple plan, but 'twas the simple ones that most often worked best.

So, no, Conan would not reveal what he had learned, not yet. He would wait. Shadizar must still be some distance away, and with only Dake and his cur to watch them, the right moment would certainly arise.

Patience was not Conan's strength, but he had learned that sometimes nothing else would serve. He would bide his time, and then he would act.

Fosull began to grow irritated at his companion's lamentations. The redheaded fat man maintained his drunkenness with a continuing influx of wine, and his babblings had become a grating upon the Varg's concentration.

Fosull himself no longer imbibed any of the wagon's contents, for it took all of his sober attention to continue his main task. The storm had done that which he had feared, smoothing the road and removing most of the wagon's tracks. Here and there, an especially deep rut remained, but those partial impressions were few and easily missed without a sharp eye. Balor's mutterings served only to distract Fosull, and he could ill afford a divided attention.

The Varg considered several options open to him. He could leave the wagon and continue his pursuit on foot. This would be slower and present the same associated risks as before. Or, he could put his spear into the fat man's heart and dump the corpse and continue on alone. Only there might be those along the way who would recognize the winejack's wagon and wonder at how a small person with muddy skin came to occupy it. Fosull had no desire to answer questions of this stripe.

Or, he could continue on as things were now, turning a mostly deaf ear to the fat man until the drunken ravings deepened into unconsciousness once again, as surely they would.

In the end, Fosull decided that the latter was the best course of action. Balor was still of more use than harm, and during a lucid moment had even told the Varg that they were fast approaching the village of Elika. Someone there might have seen the wagon, the Varg figured, and could keep him to the correct path.

So, as the sun cooked the wet earth and wrung from it the moisture of the night's storm, Fosull continued to drive the wine wagon, searching for the occasional track that belonged to the wagon of his son's captors.

Just ahead of Raseri was an open wagon drawn by oxen, working its way along the road. The Jatte shaman slowed his pace so as not to overtake the vehicle, and made to examine the conveyance and its occupants without being seen. The wagon was stacked with barrels, likely filled with wine, to judge from the faint odor of it in the air. Two small men sat upon the driver's platform, one of them apparently a child who wore a cowled robe. A father and son, likely, delivering their wares to some village farther up the road.

The wagon's speed was slower than Raseri's own, but he decided that while it offered little threat to him, it might be better to dog it for a way rather than to pass it. The giant's reason for this was simple enough: Anyone approaching from the opposite direction would likely pause and exchange greetings with the wagoneers, giving Raseri time to conceal himself did he so desire. It was a matter of giving himself more options, always a good idea. Soon enough he would have to seek answers from the small men again, as the rain had erased the tracks of the larger wagon containing his children. He hoped to find a village or a farm near one of the forks in the road so that he could make inquiry against taking the wrong path.

Keeping far enough back so that he could dart

from the road did the wagon stop, the Jatte shaman and leader followed the pair of small men.

A few moments later the larger of the two occupants crawled into the back of the wagon and disappeared from sight. Raseri worried that he had been seen, but the vehicle did not slow and it appeared that the man had not noticed him. The smaller of the men—surely a child, at that size?—continued to urge the oxen forward.

Several hours from the village, the western road from Ophir joined the wider, southerly road to Shadizar. As they approached this juncture, the sun had already begun to dry the shallower puddles along the way into traceries of cracks. There was even dust in the air ahead, a fact remarked upon by Kreg to his master.

Dake, roused from a partial slumber upon the seat, awoke fully and saw that this was indeed so. In the distance, a haze of dust did fog the air. At the same time that he noticed this, Dake also saw that the road past the melding of the highway to the distant Ophir Pass, itself just north of the border with Koth, was deeply rutted with wagon tracks and human scandal and boot prints.

"Oh-ho," Dake said. "A wealthy caravan precedes us, and only a short distance ahead."

Kreg looked at his master. "How do you know this?"

Dake said, "Did not you yourself just point out yon cloud of dust?"

"Well, aye, but—how can you tell the dust of a

wealthy caravan from that of a poor farmer driving sheep or pigs?"

Stupid, and no doubt of it. Dake sighed. "Use your wits. There are tracks of at least a dozen wagons ahead of us, as well as the prints of thrice that many men on foot. No poor farmer could manage either for driving sheep. And the tracks are fresh, laid down after the rain, and from the direction of the Ophir Pass. A simple deduction."

"True, but there could be several farmers, could there not?"

Dake sighed again. Why did he bother to explain? "Do you not recall that the Ophir Pass is thick with bandits who prey upon unwary travelers?"

"Aye."

"How much resistance do you think even a large number of dirt farmers or sheepherders would offer such brigands?"

"Not much, I expect."

"So if this group has come from that direction, then it must be protected by armed troops. Mercenaries, most likely, or mayhaps even regular soldiers. And such troops cost money; therefore, whatever they are protecting must have some value."

Watching Kreg's face was like unto watching the sun light up the morning skies. Truth dawned upon his features. "Ahhh. I see."

Hardly more than a blind man, Dake thought. And even that with as much difficulty as a goat trying to fly.

"Increase our speed," Dake said. "I would know who peoples this caravan."

Obediently Kreg stirred the oxen to a faster pace.

The sun was half through his daily journey when Fosull, still driving the wagon of the besotted and unconscious Balor, came upon the turning for the village of Elika. He would not have known this, save that a local resident was by chance arriving at that same juncture from the opposite direction at almost the same moment.

"Ho!" the man called out. "Is that Balor's wine wagon?"

"Aye," Fosull replied, "it is."

"Where then is Balor?"

Fosull had a moment to be glad he had not slain the drunkard. "He is, ah, asleep in the wagon."

The farmer laughed. "More likely soused in his own wares, I would wager"

"Just so. Tell me, friend, have you taken notice of a large wagon traveling the roads hereabout?"

"Oh, you mean Dake and his band of freaks?"

Fosull's heart sped up. "That would be it, yes."

The man shook his head sadly. " 'Twas an interesting display of oddities the freakmaster offered, but I also bet my last copper that Deri would best Dake's champion in a fighting match. Who would have known that the barbarian could move like that?"

"Would you happen to know where Dake and his band might be now?"

"On the road to Shadizar," the man said, waving

in the direction from which he had come. "Four or five hours along."

The hunting instinct in Fosull flared and he felt a surge of cold twist his bowels. Only a few hours ahead!

"One other question, friend. Are there turns that must be taken to reach this Shadizar?"

"Nay. Straight down this road as the crow flies will do it."

Fosull grinned, remembered in time that view of his teeth might cause some consternation, and managed at the last instant to keep them hidden. "I thank you. Well, we must be going."

"But are you not planning to stop at Elika and deliver some of Balor's wines?"

"To be sure, but . . . ah . . . upon our return, in a few days."

With that, Fosull snapped the reins over the back of the oxen and the wagon lurched forward. Balor did not gainsay this move, being at the moment as dead to the world as an average corpse. And if he should awaken later and offer a grumble about missing his stop, they could always part company, Fosull knew. One way or another.

Raseri watched the meeting of the wagon and the farmer from a vantage point nearer than he would have hoped for. A large clump of hedgelike bushes near the turnoff grew almost to the very edge of the road. Using care so that his great feet did not smash too many twigs or small plants, the giant was able to creep within a few spans of the wagon, to a position whereby he could hear snatches of the conversation between the driver and the pedestrian.

From the voice it was apparent that the driver of the wine wagon was no child. And a tiny flash of green under the grayish skin—not skin at all, Raseri realized—on the small man's hand gave the leader of the Jatte the final clue he needed: The driver was a Varg!

As the wagon jerked forward and began to move off, with the farmer going down the hill away from the main road, Raseri pondered this new information.

The news about the wagon, commanded by one called "Dake," was welcome of course, but what in the name of the Creator was a *Varg* doing here, so far away from home?

When the wagon was some distance down the road, far enough so that Raseri thought he might safely resume his own progress, he left the cover of the brush and started walking.

Vargs, like the Jatte, were not known to leave their home and travel among the small men. Then again, Raseri reasoned, he himself was here, having been given sufficient need. Too, the Varg must have some compelling reason to be on the road to Shadizar, following the path of those who had kidnapped three of the Jatte—

Aha!

Of a moment Raseri had a reason for the Varg's presence. The pedestrian had called the one known as "Dake" a freakmaster. Someone who displayed "oddities." A Jatte would seem an oddity, to the small men. Would not a Varg seem one also?

This Dake had taken a Varg, as well.

And as for the "barbarian" fighter of whom the farmer spoke, Raseri felt certain that this was Conan, which confirmed his earlier suspicion that his former captive was indeed in league with those who had stolen his children. And only a few hours ahead!

Raseri smiled grimly to himself. The heavier wagon would move more slowly than either the wine cart or Raseri himself. By nightfall, perhaps, he and this unknown Varg would overtake their prey.

The Jatte shaman and leader twirled the shaft of his spear reflectively in the fingers of one hand. This adventure would be finished soon, and the road would be awash in the blood of those who had caused it to begin. A Varg or two in the bargain would certainly be worth a little extra effort.

An hour after meeting the local villager, Fosull became aware that he was being followed. Taking care not to reveal this new knowledge, the Varg surreptitiously reined the feeling while pretending to check on the slumbering Balor.

Fosull saw a flash of deeply tanned skin behind him as the shadower quickly hid himself in the trees at the roadside, but the instant's view was enough to reveal that the follower was too large to be one of the outswamp men.

As Fosull turned back to his driving, he pondered what he had discovered. It was a Jatte, it had to be. No outswamp man could be that big. But—why was he following the wine wagon?

Or *was* he following the wine wagon?

Well, yes, to be sure, he was behind it and following it, after a fashion, but was that his true goal? Jatte did not leave their village very often, and then almost always in groups of three or four so as to catch the odd outswamp man. Why would a single Jatte be out here, so far away from home?

Then Fosull recalled the tracks he had seen when he had discovered the wagon's path for the first time. There were Jatte on board the same vehicle that had his son.

Of course. Someone from the giants had come to fetch back his own.

Fosull smiled, this time allowing his teeth to show since there were no outswamp men to see. Well. Perhaps he could use this to his advantage. And if not, perhaps he could manage a bit of meat for the communal pot, at the least. If he and Vilken hurried, maybe they could get home before it spoiled.

A pleasant thought.

EIGHTEEN

The first real sign that they were drawing nearer to the caravan was the appearance of rear guards who whirled about and faced Dake's wagon with lances raised. While they could hardly be called a handsome group, they were well-outfitted, with stout leather arm and shin guards, oiled chain-mail vests over thin lanate shirts, and small round shields of layered rawhide hung from wide belts. Each man bore both a short sword ensheathed at the left hip and a slim lance with a double-edged tip, more appropriate to horsemen than foot soldiers, but light and short enough to be carried easily. They all wore stout boots of good cut. Dake, who had had occasion to deal in such items from time to time, could see that the master of these men had not stinted on quality when it came to supplying them.

"Hold, there, wagoneers. Where be ye bound?"

Dake responded politely to the challenge issued by one he assumed was the leader of the six-man troop, a stocky fellow with bandy legs, red hair, a florid complexion, and squinty eyes, the latter of which were seemingly made worse by exposure to the sun's light.

"We make for Shadizar."

Squinty looked at his men, then back at Dake. "Aye, that seems reasonable, being that ye travel the Shadizar road. To what purpose?"

Dake's response was still even-toned, but slightly less polite. "Business."

"What sort of business?"

The mage's patience, never of the strongest metal, bent and nearly broke. "My business, footman, and none of yours."

Squinty seemed taken aback. He blinked, considered Dake's response for a moment, scratched at some small and unseen vermin under his chin. "Well, be that as it may, we shall be obliged to inspect your wagon."

"By what authority?"

Squinty grinned and hefted his lance. "By the authority that will have ye looking like a dart board if ye try and stop us."

Dake grinned, and it was a malevolent expression. "Well, then, by all means, inspect it."

Squinty puffed out his chest and grinned over his shoulder at his men, who nodded. He looked back at Dake. "Any women in there by chance?"

"As it happens, yes. Three."

"Hear that, boys? Women!"

The other five laughed and passed several rude remarks.

As the red-haired trooper eagerly moved toward the rear of the wagon, Dake leaned back and spoke in a low voice into the cloth that separated the passengers from the outside. "Conan, there is an ugly little man about to open the rear door. Knock him silly. Try not to kill him though."

Next to Dake, Kreg grinned.

"And the rest of you back there, there are five more fools out here on the road. When Conan clouts the one, I want you to hurry out here and catch the rest of them. They are armed, so take care that you are not speared or cut. I would like them all alive, if possible."

There was some risk, Dake knew, but it should be very slight. Were he one of the loutish guards, the sight of Dake's troop would be unnerving to say the least. He would be amazed if the five did not take to their heels with the utmost speed when they saw what they would face if they stayed. Teyle alone would frighten the wits from most men; and that combined with the sight of the others . . . well, it would take a brave man indeed to stand and fight.

Behind the wagon, the lustful Squinty reached up to open the door.

The wagon tracks were fresh, but the road upon which they lay had seen a great deal of use recently. Fosull stopped the wine cart several times and alighted to examine the various ruts and tracks, and from his observations, he deemed that a large group of wagons, horses, and men on foot had gone before the six-wheeled vehicle. Those latter tracks were deeper than the others and had characteristic nicks and grooves that Fosull had become most familiar with since he began following them.

More people would make things more difficult, Fosull realized, as he stood and dusted off his knees. A mistake, for that caused some of the dried mud on his palms to flake away, revealing the green underneath. In fact, his disguise was wearing most thin in places, and it was only Balor's constant intoxication that prevented the man from noticing.

How, Fosull wondered, did the fat man ever manage to deliver his goods when he spent so much of his time consuming them?

As the Varg climbed back onto the wagon, he looked surreptitiously back down the road for signs of his giant shadow. He did not see the Jatte but could still feel his presence out there somewhere; there was no reason to believe himself abandoned. Another problem, but one he could consider at a later time. First he had to catch up with the wagon and retrieve his son. The conveyance was only a couple of hours ahead, he reckoned, and by nightfall he might well be abreast of it.

In the back of the cart, the drunken man snored on.

* * *

Raseri did not think himself as good a tracker as the Varg, but he was adept enough to know that his quarry lay not far ahead, either in time or distance. The wheel prints were fresher, albeit somewhat harder to discern because of all the other traffic upon the road.

Well. No matter. As long as he could see them.

What to do about the Varg was another thing. It would hardly do to allow the little green animal to foul up the pursuit. Vargs had a certain low cunning, to be sure, but in matters of thought, the Jatte knew them to be lacking, on the average. Which was not to say that the Varg upon the wagon was necessarily average, of course. That he had come so far and managed to fool at least one small man into thinking he was something else was indicative of perhaps a more than rudimentary intelligence. Still, it was hardly proper for Raseri to overestimate the animal's abilities.

The Jatte waited until the wagon was far enough away as to be no more than a small dot he could hide with his thumbtip before he regained the road from his concealment in the rocks. Now and again the Varg did look back in this direction, and it was possible that the creature might have noticed that he was not alone. There was little Raseri could do about it, nor was he particularly worried about a confrontation with a single Varg armed as he himself was; still, 'twas best to keep as many options open as possible. Knowledge, as anyone with half a brain knew, was power.

Raseri strode off after the distant wagon, making alternate plans one after another, trying to serve up every possibility so that he might solve problems in advance. Chance favors a prepared mind, he knew. He was confident he could anticipate virtually everything he might encounter.

When the door to Dake's wagon was opened, Conan was ready. More than ready, he was eager to vent his anger upon anyone remotely deserving of it, and he had heard enough of the conversation between the soldier and Dake to know that the man was arrogant and altogether too officious. True, he would rather be leaping upon Dake, but failing that, being able to move and focus his rage upon another was better than nothing. So this fool would bother women, would he?

The door swung wide on its greased hinges, and a grinning red-haired man squinted into the relative darkness of the wagon.

The smile vanished as Conan leaped.

"Mitra!" the man had time to blurt before the Cimmerian was upon him.

For Conan, the scuffle was unhappily short. He swung his fist, knotted into a fleshy hammer, and slammed it into the man's left temple. The guard fell, unconscious, into a heap upon the dusty road.

Crom! He could have put up more of a fight!

Behind him, the doorway of the wagon erupted as the other passengers boiled forth and out to confront the remaining troops. Vilken was first, pointed teeth showing, followed by Penz, Oren, Morja, Tro, Sab, and last, but certainly not the least of them, Teyle.

Dake had not forbidden him to take part, Conan

realized, and with that thought, he moved. He grinned and rounded the side of the wagon, voicing a wordless cry as he did so.

At that moment Dake chose to field his red demon.

The stunned looks upon the faces of the five remaining soldiers was as sight to behold. As one unit they turned and started to flee, moving very fast indeed for men hampered with light armor.

Vilken threw his spear and hit one of the men on the unprotected part of his left hamstring; the man stumbled and went sprawling facedown.

Penz sent a loop of his rope through the air and encircled a second trooper. The noose tightened around the man's ankles, and he, too, made a sudden dive to the unforgiving road.

Conan's speed allowed him to overtake the third man, whereupon he shoved with both hands and increased the man's flight so that his legs could not keep up with his new pace. He fell and rolled, ending up on his back, yelling for mercy.

The fourth man fell clutching his head under the combined efforts of the catwoman and four-armed Sab, calling upon various gods as he did so.

The last man dodged from the road and was surrounded by Teyle and her siblings. Big she was, but her long legs gave the giant woman better than average speed once she began moving, and when the final trooper found himself running toward the Jatte woman, he threw down his lance and held his palms out toward her in surrender.

Conan could understand that he and his companions would appear to be formidable, to be sure, but he felt a sense of disgust at how easily the troops had been taken. Whoever paid these six was surely not getting his money's worth.

"Bring them back here," Dake ordered. "I feel that we shall make quite an impression on the caravan when we arrive bearing its rear guards trussed up like pigs for the slaughter!"

There were other guards of course, armed as those now marching in front of Dake's wagon had been. But their amazement at seeing their fellows bound around the arms and shoulders, only their legs free for walking, caused no small stir when finally the entire assemblage arrived at the main body of the caravan.

The caravan was as rich as Dake had forecast. Wagons covered with white and red tents held the center of the train. One of the wagons was larger than Dake's own. The smell of perfume wafted over the sweat stink of the footmen and horses, and the air was also laden with the scent of spice. He heard the soft voices of women coming from one of the larger wagons. The freakmaster would wager that whatever was in the cargo wagons was worth no small amount in the main bazaar at Shadizar.

The line of armed men, at least a score and a half strong, leveled their lances uneasily. Some of the guards made warding-off signs against curses and the evil eye.

"Here, what deviltry is this?" a large trooper called out.

Behind the captured soldiers, Dake stood on the

wagon's driving platform and engaged his best voice. "I would speak to your master!"

In due course, a tall and regal man, swathed in the finest blue Aquilonian silk robes and head-dress, appeared and moved imperiously toward Dake's wagon. Upon his feet were boots cut from the skins of large desert lizards, and he wore a neatly trimmed full beard, mostly black but shot through with gray, and his nose was nearly a beak under steely blue eyes. A cruel and arrogant face, Dake saw, belonging to a man of wealth and power, the face of one used to getting his way.

Excellent!

"I am the master of this caravan and of those men you have mistreated," the man said, his voice a deep baritone. "Who are you to trifle with my servants?"

Dake, wise in the ways of rich men, knew when to bluster and when to flatter. His voice took on an obsequious tone. "I? I am merely Dake the freakmaster, O great lord. I travel to Shadizar seeking a patron to sponsor the most incredible collection of oddities known to man. I thought only to demonstrate how unworthy these so-called guards are for a man of your obvious greatness."

The caravan master glared at the trussed guards. "Well, that they are unworthy is obvious enough." Then, "*Freak*master?"

Dake stuck his hand through the curtain and gestured. After a moment his thralls emerged from the back of the wagon again, to the gasps and won-derment of the caravan.

"Behold for yourself, my Lord . . . ?"

"Capeya," the caravan master finished. "And not a lord, but only a simple . . . merchant."

"Ah, a man who *earned* his wealth rather than inherited it."

Capeya smiled, showing strong teeth. "Just so, friend Dake." He looked at the freaks as they drew nearer; he was obviously impressed. "Quite an assembly. I have never seen such a variety, even in Shadizar during the High Festival. A unique collection."

"Just so," Dake said, his own smile more than a match for Capeya's.

"These will draw large crowds when displayed."

"And they are even more than they appear, good merchant." Dake strove to make the word "merchant" sound as much like "milord" as he could. " 'Twas they who subdued the six rear guards with what I must confess was little effort."

"Ah. Even better." Capeya smiled again. "And you are seeking a sponsor, you say?"

"In a word, yes."

"My wagon is appointed in a somewhat comfortable fashion, friend Dake. Perhaps you might join me there to partake of some not-unworthy vintage wine I have recently obtained? We might then speak of things that might be to our . . . mutual benefit."

Dake's joy was unbounded. Finding this caravan was a stroke of fortune almost beyond belief. Shadizar was still days away but he already had a patron, he did not doubt it for a moment, could they but come to terms!

He kept his face bland when he responded.

"Why, certainly I should enjoy that, friend Capeya." Inwardly he grinned like a slackwit. He had never met a merchant who could out-bargain him, and he did not think Capeya would be an exception.

Here, he knew, was the first stop on the road to riches!

NINETEEN

Conan liked it not that Dake seemed to get along so well with the master of the caravan. Alike as two fleas on an alley rat they were, and the Cimmerian could sense a rogues' alliance already aborning. This did not help matters of possible escape. True, should he break free of the curse Dake had laid upon him, he felt he could win through the guards easily enough. He had his sword, and his recent experience with the merchant's small army impressed him little. To a motley collection of hill bandits, these troops would likely appear to be a threat, whereas Conan recognized them for layabouts who looked better than they were. Carving a path through such men would entail some dangers, to be sure, but not enough to worry over-much about. He was, after all, composed of somewhat sterner stuff than the average hill bandit. He did not have to best them all, only one or two who stood directly between him and freedom.

For the others, especially the children, things might not be so easy, however, and Conan resolved that he would not go off and leave them behind as Dake's captives. Despite her earlier trickery, Teyle had proven to be a friend, with her ministrations to his wounds and what other comforts she offered in the night. Conan had forgiven her her transgression against him. She had learned her lesson about being a slave, and he was not so small of mind as to deny a repentant woman another chance. She certain could not depart without her younger brother and sister, and as long as he was bringing three, he might as well bring the rest. Besides, he had grown to like the group; despite their unusual appearance, they were far better men and women than Dake and his cur. Penz was an ugly freak but kindhearted; Kreg was a handsome fellow, but evil to his rotten core. There was a lesson in recognizing this.

Conan marched alongside the freakmaster's wagon, the dust kicked up by the men, animals, and wagons ahead of him filling the air, adding to the dirt of his sweaty skin and making it difficult to breathe. The other thralls fared little better, save perhaps for Teyle, who was tall enough to avoid ingesting much of the disturbed road grit. Would that he had a bath of hot spring water. Might as well wish for a palace of rubies while you are at it, Conan.

Kreg drove the wagon, looking angry. Perhaps

he resented being left behind while Dake went to drink and dine with the merchant. Good. Any small discomfort Kreg had to suffer raised Conan's spirits. Maybe the lackey would stab his master in the back in irritation. Stranger things had happened.

Since Dake was occupied some distance away, this might be an ideal time to try an escape, save that it was still daylight and such an attempt would be all too obvious. Conan did not doubt his abilities to overcome a sentry or two once he was free, but were he slowed by his struggle to break the spell, Kreg might well have enough time to plant a spear in his back, or have one of the merchant's troopers do so. He was, after all, the least valuable member of the enthralled collection, and therefore expendable.

So the Cimmerian trudged along, biding his time. Sooner or later that time would arrive, and he would be certain to be ready when it did.

Fosull was surprised when he realized what had happened. In truth, it had never occurred to him that the kidnappers of his son intended to join the collection of wagons further up the road. He knew little of the ways of the outswamp men, and had thought those of the large group ahead of them to be no more than fellow travelers going in the same direction. By the Green God's left testicle, this surely complicated matters!

"Wh-where are we?"

Fosull glanced around to see Balor struggling to sit up, clutching his head with one hand.

"On the road. Other than that, I know not.'

The fat man managed to purchase a sitting pose. He glanced around. "Bu-but this is well past the village!"

"We stopped there this morning," Fosull lied. "Do you not recall?"

"We did?"

"Certainly. You sold two casks of wine and then gambled the money away betting upon a race between two beetles."

"No!"

"Indeed."

Balor started to shake his head, moaned at this, and stopped, now gripping his skull with both hands. "I recall none of it. Was I drunk?"

"Aye. You drank a dozen flagons of wine."

"Only a dozen? Odd, that normally would not cause me to lose my memory."

"That was before the race. Afterward you drank a dozen more."

"Ah. That must explain it."

"Perhaps you might drink a bit more now, since it seems you are afflicted with some malady."

"Hair of the dog that bit me for a cure, eh? Not a bad idea. What did you say your name was again, small friend?"

Fosull could not stop his grin in time.

Balor's eyes grew wide. "I think maybe I have had too much wine, friend. I am seeing things."

"Wine is the cure for many illnesses, is it not?"

"You do have a point. And you are kind to drive my wagon while I attempt to heal myself. I shall reward you in Shadizar. If I survive that far."

With that, Balor lay back down and reached for one of the smaller kegs.

Fosull still had his main problem, though. His prey had become enveloped in a very large collection of like folk, and that put a different face on how he would manage to recover his son and deal his foes justice. Perhaps he could leave off the justice portion and simply recover Vilken? As he reckoned it, he was no more than an hour behind the wagons, and it would be dark soon. Night was a friend to the Vargs back in the swamps, and Fosull did not think it would be less so here. Much could be done under the cover of darkness that would fail under the sun's harsh eyes, especially when none knew he was about.

Of course, there was that cursed Jatte dogging his tracks; *he* knew of Fosull's existence. To be caught between the many hands of the outswamp men and a Jatte was not high among Fosull's worldly desires. Something would have to be done about the giant, without a doubt. And soon, too.

Suddenly a thought pierced the clouds of Fosull's mind, a thought so stunning as to nearly unseat him from the wagon. It blossomed like a toadstool after a hard rain, invisible one moment, there the next, and it was so incredible as to nearly overwhelm him. Simply, yes, believable, hardly, and yet . . . and yet it could be the solution to retrieving his son *and* dealing with the Jatte.

Fosull grinned, no longer worried that Balor might see his pointed teeth. His proposal was a thing no Varg had ever done before, so audacious was it, but it appealed to him. After all, was he not

Fosull, bravest and cleverest of all his kind? Would it not be fitting that he be the first to ever attempt something so radical?

Aye, he decided. It would be fitting.

Of course it could also be fatal, but without risks, life held little meaning.

By all the gods, he would do it!

When the six-wheeled wagon tracks began to be partially obscured by others, Raseri knew he was confronted by a new set of difficulties. His quarry now rode with a rather numerous escort of its own kind, and that boded ill for the leader of the Jatte. To be sure, he had raised that possibility in his mind earlier, but it had been dismissed as not being very likely until they reached a settlement. That had been a miscalculation, and Raseri was not one to suffer such things gladly.

"The Creator's lowest curse upon you all!" he said under his breath.

So intent was Raseri upon his misjudging that he paid less than full attention to his tracking task. He reasoned that as long as he could see the wine cart there in the distance, there was no real need to be overly assiduous, but this proved to be another error.

Out of the thin brush next to the road to his left, the hooded form of the Varg suddenly appeared, brandishing his spear.

"Hold, Jatte!"

Raseri swung his own spear around and hefted it in preparation for a throw. "Are you mad, Varg, to dare face me alone?" Raseri made ready to skewer the little green beast. He drew back his arm—

"Nay, stay your cast, Jatte."

This surprised Raseri. "Why should I?"

"We trail the same quarry."

"What of it?"

"They have taken my son, Vilken."

"That matters not bug's dung to me."

"But they have also taken three of your people."

Raseri reminded himself that knowledge was power. He lowered his spear arm slightly. "You have seen them?"

"Nay. But I saw the tracks earlier, back along the road, so they still live."

"Praise the Creator for that," Raseri said. Then, "Why did you stop and confront me, about-to-be-dead Varg?"

"I want my son back. You want your own back. There are many of them and only one each of us."

"This is true. So?"

"I propose a . . . temporary alliance."

Raseri was tempted to laugh, but the statement intrigued him. He lowered his spear a little more. "An alliance? Jatte with Varg? You must be mad."

"Each of us has certain abilities the other does not. You are much more powerful, but I can hide in places you cannot. You are clever in ways different than I. I am agile, and you are strong. Would we not stand a better chance of accomplishing our respective tasks together than separate?"

Raseri lowered his spear so that the butt rested on the ground. He stared at the Varg, amazed.

"You are passing clever for an animal. I must concede that you have a point."

The Varg lowered his own spear and grinned, showing his wicked teeth. "You are considering my proposition, then?"

"Nay. I have already considered it. It makes sense, though I am not inclined to trust you."

"If I give my word as leader of the Vargs to offer you no danger until after our people are rescued, would that suffice?"

"You are the leader of the Vargs?"

The little green creature drew himself up to his full height, such that it was. "I am. Fosull, I am called."

"Well, I will be dipped in goat dung. I am Raseri, shaman and chief of the Jatte."

"Then we have a truce?"

Raseri paused for a moment. He could squash the Varg at any time, should it prove necessary. Meanwhile, the little beast had a logical point that could not be denied.

"We have a truce."

"Good. Let us go then, Raseri, and find a way to recover our own."

"Lead on, Fosull."

Raseri was not quite ready to turn his unprotected back on the Varg, but he was quite amazed. That a Varg would have the sense to think of such a thing was beyond any experience that Jatte had ever had of Vargs. He had underestimated these little green beasts, and badly.

Would wonders never cease?

* * *

Dake could feel the admittedly excellent wine working upon him, but its effect only made his wits quicker. The transaction was essentially complete; all that remained now was to fill in the final details. The meat of the bargain was, he felt, mainly his. In exchange for the merchant's not-inconsiderable protection and patronage, Dake would tender to him one quarter of the profits gained from display and other uses of the freaks. After operating expenses, of course. And the day that Dake could not conceal the amount of such profits by fifteen percent in his favor, he would dance naked through the streets of Shadizar with a rancid goat draped over his shoulders.

"And as to the breeding procedures . . . ?" Capeya asked, rather delicately.

"How do you mean, my partner?"

"Could we not . . . ah . . . charge admission to watch?"

Dake covered his smile with a sip of wine from the carved wooden cup. This merchant was perhaps more clever than he appeared. His suggestion was an excellent idea.

Dake said so, eliciting a smile and nod in return.

"And I must say that the idea of this . . . circus, as you call it, a large circle filled with attractions, has a certain merit. I have also properties in the city of Arenjun, as well as some small holdings in the neighboring country of Khauran, to the southeast, which might stand conversion to smaller replicas of this, provided you can produce enough of your oddities to people them."

"Never fear, good man; that I can surely do. I

am not without certain . . . magical skills that will ensure just what I say."

"Excellent. I foresee a long and profitable association, Dake, my friend."

"As do I. Let us drink, then, to your continued good health."

"And to yours."

The two men drank deeply of the wine.

Capeya put his cup down and clapped his hands twice.

A young woman draped revealingly in red silks entered the tent, disturbing the balance of the moving wagon only sightly.

"This is one of my slaves," the merchant said. "To use as you will."

"Why, you are most kind, good man. Perhaps you would enjoy a . . . visitation with one of my more comely thralls? It would be the least I could do."

The merchant's eyes took on a sudden gleam. "Ah, yes. The giantess, the younger sister, she reminds me of one of my daughters. I could find things to say to her."

Dake grinned, as one man of the world to another.

"Doubtless, doubtless. Tonight, then, when the wagons are still, I shall have her brought to you for your pleasure."

"You are a generous man."

"No more than yourself."

The two smiled at each other again, but Dake's was the larger grin. Aha, he thought. You have revealed a weakness to me, my new partner. I shall not forget that you are a molester of children.

Not that Dake cared a whit for the girl's fate. He would have taken her himself earlier, save that it had not been convenient. Perhaps he would attend to that before he sent the girl to the merchant's wagon.

Dake smiled, and the expression was full of all manner of things.

TWENTY

Night scattered her stars across the skies like bright grains of sand, tiny pinpricks through the curtain of darkness to the pure white beyond. A gibbous moon waxed near to full, bathing in pale silver the land, casting cool shadows in eerie shapes. Far from the abodes of man, and with no more than cooking fires to disturb the night, the caravan stood halted, the draft animals grazing on what vegetation they could find.

Conan returned to the wagon from the call of nature, taking in the sights and smells of the camp and evening. Were he free, this was the kind of place in which he felt most at ease. The quiet night did not have the call of a busy town, no inns at which to drink or wench, but it had a grace of its own.

As he moved the wagon, he saw a flash of gray under the bright moon, someone moving into concealment behind a scrubby clump of brush not far away from where he walked.

While the Cimmerian's eyes were as sharp as any man's, they could not penetrate the bush sufficiently to reveal what lay within. The figure that had darted behind the cover was small, childlike, but Conan felt that there was another, larger person also concealed there, though he could not have said exactly why he felt this.

He would have investigated but he was under magical orders to attend to his functions and return to the wagon, and the wards were too powerful to try on such a casual curiosity.

Inside, there were other problems more pressing.

Morja sat quietly sobbing in one corner of the wagon. She was attended by Teyle, who glanced up with pain in her eyes as Conan returned. Dake meant to send the girl to the merchant for the man's perverted pleasure, and there was nothing any of them could do to stop it. Impotent rage filled the wagon; all within were seething at the prospect.

To the catwoman Conan said quietly, "Ask Dake for permission to leave the wagon. When you pass it, look carefully at the large bush that grows thirty or so paces to the left."

Tro looked puzzled.

"Someone hides there, and I would know who."

She nodded and moved to the front of the wagon to speak through the curtain to Dake.

After the catwoman left, Conan moved to confer with Teyle.

"We cannot allow this to happen," she said, her voice tight and brittle. "She is but a child!"

Conan nodded. "Mayhap we can do something."

Her look of hope touched the Cimmerian's young heart. "What?"

He started to tell her of his belief that sufficiently powerful rage could break the spell.

Dake stuck his head into the wagon at that moment and interrupted them. "I go to enjoy my new benefactor's largess," he said. "A lush woman in red silks awaits my pleasure." He looked at the still-crying Morja. "Kreg shall come for you in a few moments. Stop that crying—no, wait, continue it. It will add spice to Capeya's enjoyment of you, unless I miss my guess."

He looked around at the others. "The rest of you behave yourselves quietly until I return in the morning."

With that, Dake was gone.

"Conan?"

To the giantess he said, "Wait a moment."

Kreg arrived, grinning. "Come along, big little girl. Tonight you learn how to be a woman."

Teyle lunged after her sister as Kreg led her from the wagon, but it was as if she struck an invisible wall. Dake had taken pains to instruct each of them not to try to stop Kreg.

Tro returned.

"Conan!" Teyle said, her voice cracking.

"I understand your fear," he said, "but bide a moment." To the catwoman he said, "Well?"

"There are two men there. One is very small, Vilken's size. The other is like Teyle, even larger."

"Father!" Both Vilken and Oren spoke as one.

Conan grinned. Good. The more confusion, the better. To the other slaves he said, "Attend closely! I think we can break free of Dake's spell. And we must hurry, if we are to save Morja."

"The one like a cat saw us," Fosull said.

"Perhaps not," Raseri said. "Else there would have been an outcry raised."

"Not if she is a prisoner like the others. I think perhaps the only one free is that lout with the straw-colored hair. And the dark one, of course. Dake."

"Is it not odd that neither she nor the barbarian man tried to escape? None watched them as they came and went. What would have stopped them from simply walking away?"

The Varg shook his head. "I know not. It is as you say, decidedly odd."

Raseri mused on this point for a moment. Then he said, "Well. Both this Dake and the straw-haired man are gone, and that girl with the latter is my daughter, Morja! We should free those in the wagon first and then go after her."

"Agreed. I am less likely to be seen. You keep watch and I shall approach the wagon."

"That seems reasonable."

Fosull took a deep breath, let it out, and started for the wagon in which his son was imprisoned.

* * *

Inside the peaked canopy that covered the pillow-strewn conveyance, Dake leaned back on a thick cushion and allowed the comely slave to pour him another flagon of excellent wine. He sipped at the liquid, then smiled at the young woman. She smiled nervously in return, and the flickering of the tapers set here and there inside the tent illuminated a comely face.

"I would see what you look like under those silks," Dake said. "Remove them."

The girl did so, and the mage was not unimpressed by what she revealed. Her skin was of a tawny shade, and unblemished, and she was heavy of breast and wide of hip, a body made for a man's pleasure, he reckoned.

"Come closer," Dake said, grinning.

Conan felt the simmering anger of the others around him begin to boil, as did his own. To be slaves, to be forced to obey Dake's every whim, it was intolerable!

For a barbarian, accustomed to uncomplicated emotions, it was not a difficult task to allow one's rage to burst forth. But if Conan thought that the others held less anger than his own, he quickly realized that he was mistaken.

Penz seemed to glow with anger, his eyes wide and his lips skinned back to reveal his long eye-teeth.

Tro and Sab shook with their emotion, the woman growling softly deep in her throat, the four-armed man clenching and unclenching all of his hands into tight fists.

Spittle flew from Vilken's mouth as he chanted something over and over, toneless words Conan did not understand.

Teyle merely stared at the place where last she had seen her sister, but her face was flushed and her breathing came fast and loud.

Even the giant boy, Oren, seemed about to sunder apart from pressures inside his body.

Conan felt the rage gathering as a tangible thing, a thickening of the very air around them into dark emotion, as if the wagon had become filled with black smoke.

It grew, stronger and stronger, until Conan knew he must move . . . or die.

"Now!" he yelled. "Now!"

Fosull was nearly to the wagon when suddenly it flew apart, as if it were a melon dropped upon hard ground. The door to the rear burst open and was ripped from its hinges as the large barbarian sailed forth—

Another man followed the barbarian; no, it was a young Jatte, screaming something incoherent—

The heavy canvas of upper wall shredded under the claws of the wolfman, and he dived through the opening, howling—

Through the front of the wagon came the cat-woman and a man with four arms, both plummeting to the ground and rolling up to stand again—

Vilken—*Vilken!*—sliced open another section of the canvas with his spear and leaped forth, yelling the Suicide Attack Chant at the top of his voice—

The giant woman stood and burst the roof with

her hands, tearing the heavy cloth as if it were a spider's web, yelling in a booming voice for someone named Morja!

Fosull stood stunned under the onslaught of activity, unable to think of what to say or do.

"This way!" came the deep voice of Raseri, a sound surely loud enough to disturb the sleep of the dead.

Fosull turned and saw that the escapees had also heard the roar.

"Father!" Fosull heard Vilken call. "I knew you would come for me!"

Fosull turned and saw his son. He managed a quick smile. "Aye, boy. But I planned to do it with less noise! We must be away, quickly!"

"Is that a *Jatte* with you?"

"We shall speak of it later. Your own companions are no less strange."

"True, Father. True."

Fosull turned and ran toward the spot from whence Raseri beckoned. The sounds from the wagon must have alerted the entire caravan—men were stirring and yelling in wonderment—and the plan of sneaking away quietly was destroyed. Best to leave quickly now, and a spear to anyone who stood in the way!

Dake was groaning under the practiced hands and lips of the naked slave when suddenly he felt something snap in his mind. For a moment he confused the feeling with that of pleasure, but it quickly became apparent that the cause was other than that.

His thralls had slipped away from his control!

The mage leaped up from the cushions and shoved the surprised woman away, cursing as he moved.

"M-m-milord?"

"Silence, woman! Where are my clothes?"

As Dake scrabbled about, searching for his robe and boots, he felt the presence of his freaks dwindling with every passing moment. What had happened? His spell had never been broken before! How could this be? Was it Capeya? Did he have some wizardry Dake had not noticed? Was this some treachery on the merchant's part?

Dake hurriedly dressed and leaped from the wagon. He needed answers, and fast.

Outside, the camp was in turmoil. Men yelled at each other in the dark, cursed as they stumbled about, trying to determine what was happening, and got in Dake's way as he raced for his wagon, calling for Kreg.

What in the name of the Seven Hells had happened?

Conan ran for all he was worth and still could not maintain the pace of Teyle, who ran ahead of him.

The spell was shattered, they were free, but he kept his sword at the ready in case he should encounter Dake along the way. The mage might be able to recast his magic, and Conan meant to give him cold and sharp iron before he could muster his wits to try it.

Ahead, Teyle yelled for her sister . . . and got an

answer as Morja called back to her as from a distance.

The running man lost sight of the giantess as she rounded a collection of wagons. He was slowed further when two men bounded into his path, holding their short swords ready for battle.

The Cimmerian was moving too fast to even try to dodge round them. He swung his blade back and forth, hard.

The two had badly underestimated Conan's speed. Their own cuts were too slow, and the broadsword's song was joined by the sound of the head of the guard on the left being severed from his neck, and the arm of the guard on the right being sheared above the elbow.

The slashes slowed Conan only slightly, and while one man screamed and the other man's head tried to, the Cimmerian thundered past.

He caught sight of Teyle just as she reached Kreg. The blond man had released his grip on Morja and was attempting to draw his long dagger when Teyle slapped at him. Her open hand caught Dake's cur across the face, smashing his nose and causing him to turn a three-quarter backward somersault to lie sprawled upon the ground.

He would be unconscious or dead from the force of that blow, Conan knew.

"Teyle!"

The giantess turned and saw Conan bearing down on her.

"She is all right," Teyle said. "They had yet to reach the merchant's wagon."

"Good. Let us leave, now!"

Teyle and Morja nodded, and turned to follow Conan.

They were free, but it would do them little good were they slain by the remaining guards. Even such dullards as those would be difficult to face in enough numbers, and Conan was not ready to die, not so shortly after regaining his freedom.

They ran to find the others who had escaped.

TWENTY-ONE

It was a strange collection indeed that left the confines of the merchant's caravan under the waxing moon. Conan, aided by the keen vision of a catwoman and the sharp nostrils of a wolfman, led four giants, two green dwarves, and a four-armed man away from imminent slaughter.

They passed a small wagon in which a fat man sat cradling his head. When the rotund one looked up and saw the group, Conan heard him moan and say something about drinking too much wine.

The Cimmerian set and kept up a goodly pace, for he did not know if they would be followed, and if so, when such pursuit might commence. Ordinarily it was risky to chase anyone in the dark, and despite the nearly full moon, it was not wise to move quickly over unknown ground at speed.

Conan's first instinct had been to leave the road and move across the mesa-like flat ground—there was no point in making the chase easy, did it come.

He thought that Dake would certainly wish to recapture them. They had been, after all, his livelihood, and of a moment, were so no longer. Too, Dake would be greatly angered. Conan's captivity had shown him that the man could not stand to be thwarted in any way; certainly this was a major attack on the freakmaster's pride.

"Take care," Tro said. "There is a dip in the ground ahead."

Conan pulled his thoughts away from pursuit and scanned the darkness. Yes, he saw the depression, to the left. He veered to the right to avoid it.

"I didn't see anything," Oren observed.

"That's because you are a stupid, blind meat animal," Vilken said.

"Oh? And you are less than dog dung!"

"Silence!" came the voices of Raseri and Fosull together.

Conan grinned, and continued to move further into the night.

It was good that Dake's magicks were of a small order, for were his stares able to destroy, there would exist nothing more than a smoking crater for as far as eye could see.

Sitting on the ground by the freakmaster's feet, Kreg cupped his hands around his smashed nose. The bleeding had stopped, but the man's handsome face would never be the same.

"On your feet, fool! We must go after them!"

Kreg gripped the wheel of the wagon next to which he sat and clambered upward. "In the dark?"

"In a firestorm from Gehanna if need be!"

Dake turned to where Capeya stood waiting. "Does that present a problem? You now own one quarter of the profit of those who have escaped."

"Aye, and I would see them recovered. This area is unafflicted with bandits. We can leave a dozen men to watch the caravan and take twice that number for pursuit."

"You yourself would join the chase?"

Capeya grinned. "Aye. I am not unfamiliar with hunting. I have slain tusked pigs and musk oxen. Men die easier than either."

Dake nodded, but inwardly he did not agree. Pigs and wild bulls might be fierce, but they did not have the cunning of men, nor did they throw spears or swing swords. Still, he had but to get close to the escapees and they would fall under his control again. This time he would remain vigilant until they could be conventionally imprisoned in a suitable enclosure with sufficient guards to watch over them. Their escape had been a fluke, likely caused by his distraction with the slave girl.

"How soon can we leave?" Drake asked.

"Within the half hour, or I shall know why."

"Good."

As Capeya's men gathered themselves and their gear for the chase, Dake collected several items of his own from his wagon. He had a few more spells that might prove useful on the trail, and he packed carefully the magical implements he would need to perform those conjures. If need be, he could field the rain of toads and the demon, but those would hardly be potent against his thralls, since they knew the illusionary nature of the amphibians and red giant.

That he would recover the escapees the magician did not doubt. They were on foot and ill-supplied, and it would be only a matter of time. He would have to take care to avoid injuring the more valuable ones whilst securing them within his spell's range, but some of them were less valuable than others. Conan the barbarian had outlived his usefulness, for one. The man was dangerous. It was he who had killed one guard and gravely wounded another during the escape; the sooner he was dead, the better.

An hour away from captivity, Conan paused long enough to meet more formally his new companions. Teyle had explained to her father something of how they had come to be captured, exonerating Conan.

For the Cimmerian there was no joy in seeing the leader of the Jatte again. He would as soon spit the giant on his blade as look at him, but for now, at least, Raseri was much less of a danger than Dake and his newfound henchmen.

Fosull was introduced by Vilken as his father.

Were he in their position, Conan knew that he too would have gone after his own children; no man worthy of the name would do otherwise. Still, he would prefer to be far away from this entire collection of folk, given his choice.

The choice was hardly his to make at the moment. True, he could leave and perhaps circle widely around the caravan and continue onward to Shadizar. Although this merchant, Capeya, was apparently fairly well placed there, the city was also supposedly large enough for a man to lose himself within. He might stay there months, or years, without meeting the merchant or his hirelings again. Conan, however, was not a man who liked to sleep with one eye open, and knowing that he would have to avoid being discovered by Capeya grated upon him. It would be like having a sharp pebble inside one's boot, forever annoying until it was removed. Until he decided what he wished to do about it, this was as good a place to be as any.

Raseri said, "We cannot lead them to our homes."

"Agreed," Fosull said.

Conan shook his head. "Dake already knows where your people live. You have help there. Your reasoning makes no sense."

"Would this Dake have told the others?" Fosull asked.

"Not likely," Penz said. "He gives away nothing of value."

"Well, then, if we slay him and his assistant, there will be no one to reveal our location," Raseri said.

Conan looked at the group. "We have one sword, three spears—two of them rather short—and a coil of rope. That is hardly enough weaponry to overcome twenty or thirty well-armed troops, albeit badly trained ones."

"We would have surprise on our side," Fosull said.

"Aside from the odds," Conan continued, "your problem would still exist if you *did* slay Dake and Kreg."

Raseri looked at Conan, and his expression was a shrewd one, the Cimmerian saw.

"I do not understand," Teyle said.

"*We* know of your village," Conan said. He waved at Tro, Sab, and Penz.

"But what of it?" the giantess asked.

"They are not Jatte, daughter."

"Nor Varg," Fosull added.

Teyle faced her father directly. "Father, it was Conan who was responsible for freeing us. It was Conan who came to help me free Morja. And it was Conan who resisted Dake more than any of us."

"None of which makes him Jatte, daughter."

"So you would slay him and the others for the crime of not being Jatte?" She turned toward Fosull. "Or Varg?"

"For the crime of knowing where to find us."

"Are we to hide for the rest of our lives and the lives of our children's children? As the outswamp men grow in numbers and reach, is it not inevitable that they shall someday stumble across us?"

"Mayhaps. Death is inevitable too, but it is to be put off as long as possible."

As father and daughter spoke, Conan quietly drew his sword. Raseri noticed this, and reached for his spear.

"Then let us decide who lives and who dies now," Conan said.

Raseri grabbed his weapon and started to come up, as did both Fosull and Vilken.

Penz, Tro, and Sab tensed and made ready to attack or defend.

"No!" Teyle yelled.

Raseri spared her a glance. "It must be so, daughter."

"I have come to know these people as my friends," she said. "If you would slay them, then slay me, too."

"You have lost your senses!"

"No. I have gained them."

Oren and Morja moved to stand next to Teyle. "She is right, Father," the girl said. "They are our friends, too."

"You have all gone mad," the Jatte leader said, shaking his head.

"What of you, Vilken?" Fosull asked.

"I would not oppose you, Father, but for meat animals, they have acted quite well."

"Best listen to your children," Conan said. "For if this fight does not go your way and we survive, you will have died for no good reason."

Conan held his sword loosely, ready to swing it into play if need be. The bones of the Jatte were exceedingly hard, as he had reason to know, but the point of his blade would certainly pierce their flesh, and he intended to skewer Raseri's heart if the giant lifted the butt of his spear from the ground. The giant was strong, but the Cimmerian knew he was faster. He gathered his strength for the leap.

Raseri stood silent for what seemed a long time. Then he said, "There is among my kind a potion that induces forgetfulness; it fogs the memory of recent events. If we survive this encounter with Dake and his ilk, would the four of you be willing to drink of the potion?"

Conan looked at the man with the face of a wolf, the woman with the features of a cat, and the four-armed man. Each of them nodded. Like it or not, he had become their leader, and they were deferring to him.

Conan faced Raseri again. "If you can offer proof that this potion is not merely a poison, we would consider it."

"I am willing to drink of it myself before you do," Raseri said. "Is that sufficient proof?"

"Along with your word that it will only fog our memories, aye."

"You have my word."

"Very well. But if you have such a substance, why have you not administered it to others before and allowed them to go free?"

"I did not trust it. Who knows but that the effect might wear off over the course of a long life?"

"But you are willing to trust it now?"

"Rather than fight with my own children? Yes."

Conan nodded. "If we survive, then."

Penz said, "Listen!"

Conan strained his ears but could not hear what had disturbed the wolfman.

"Men approach," Penz said. "And horses."

"Best we move," Conan said. "We can discuss all this later, but here is not a place to stage a defense."

"Agreed," Raseri said.

Fosull turned to his son. "Go ahead and find us such a place. Quickly!"

Vilken hurried into the darkness, and the rest of them moved out after him.

"Tracks, milord," said the trooper.

From the back of the fine horse upon which he rode, Dake recognized the man as the squinty-eyed one who had stopped him on the road.

The freakmaster turned to the merchant. "I would have thought you would have had this one gutted for his inefficiency."

"Aye, I would have, save that despite his lack of wit, he is our best tracker."

"A pity."

"Is not that always the way of it? Adequate help is so difficult to find and keep."

Dake glanced over at Kreg, who still attended to his smashed nose. Aye, that was the truth of all gods.

The merchant asked, "What do the tracks tell us?"

Squinty had two men with torches bending over the ground, and he returned to his own inspection of the soft dirt. After another few moments, he stood and approached his master.

"There be ten of them, milord. Four of 'em big and heavy, one of 'em even bigger than the giant woman. Two of 'em be very small—likely the green froggy one has another like him along. The rest be normal-sized."

Dake considered this information. So, another giant and another of the dwarves had arrived. Interesting. They might have carried with them some kind of counterspell that had freed the others. Only, Dake did not think it so. Were they wizards of note, they would likely have opted to inflict more damage rather than to flee. That they had followed him for such a lengthy distance was amazing. They were tenacious. That was important to know too.

Odd that they would have joined together, since according to Vilken's information, the two peoples hated each other. That might be a bad sign, too.

Ah, well. There was nothing to be done for it. He was not willing to turn back and give up his entire stock of wealth in the world. At the worst, even salvaging a few of the freaks would be better than none at all.

"Let us find them," Dake said. "They cannot be too far ahead. If good fortune is with us, we shall have them back before another day had passed."

Forward they rode.

TWENTY-TWO

Vilken returned to the hurrying group after a few minutes to report to his father.

"There is no high ground in this direction," he said. "All is flat, with scrub growth scarcely able to hide a rabbit, much less all of us. If we turn to the south, we might reach the rocky outcrops by dawn."

"We are no more than half an hour ahead of them," Conan observed. "They move slower in the dark, having to track us, but doubtless shall increase their pace once it is light."

"Have you any suggestions?" Raseri said.

"Aye. Move toward the hills. The rocky ground there will better hide our trail. And we might prepare ways to slow them, if we hurry."

No one had any better ideas, so they agreed to Conan's plan, tenuous though it was.

Raseri felt as if he were in control of the situation as well as could be expected. One of his main goals, to retrieve his children, had been achieved. The other part of his mission, to destroy those who knew the location of the Jatte village, lay nearly within his grasp. He had spoken only half the truth to his daughter earlier. Death was to be put off for as long as possible, unless that death served a higher purpose. Could he make certain none knew how to find his people, then he was willing to pay for that with whatever coin it required, even his own life.

Conan must die, as must the three freaks, and those who had held his children captives. If this was not accomplished in the fight that must soon be waged, then it would be achieved afterward.

There might be such things as potions that would fog memory, but were there, Raseri of the Jatte did not know of them. He did, however, know how to brew a dozen poisons from common herbs, leaves, or flowers, and he would make such a drink for any survivors among those who must die.

He had given his word, to be certain, but a promise given to an enemy was meaningless in Raseri's ethical system. Protecting his people was more important than anything else. He was the shaman and leader, and this was his highest duty, no matter what the cost. He need only survive long enough to ensure his people's safety, and he thought himself rather clever to have avoided a direct confrontation with Conan and the freaks until he could guarantee the destruction of anybody who might be a danger.

Fosull would have left with Vilken had he thought his chances to return home were better that way. Although he did not trust any of his companions save his son, he saw them as his best protection were there to be an attack. In the confusion, he and Vilken could escape. Already he had coated the tip of his spear with the juice of the *glit* berry, a fast-acting poison that would fell a victim in only a few heartbeats. Normally a hunter would avoid using the poison, for it made the meat of whatever it killed inedible, but in matters of self-defense, eating was less important than breathing.

As the group worked its way through the dwindling darkness toward the rocks yet ahead of them, Fosull considered which of his potential enemies might be first to take a spear, should it come to that. Raseri was the strongest, and likely the most dangerous—Fosull had seen a Jatte throw a spear and impale a Varg at over a hundred of his paces— but Conan could not be discounted. He was fast, and according to Vilken's stories of their captivity, told in hushed tones as they walked, more than passing strong himself. Nor was the giantess to be ignored, for she could kill a Varg with a punch or kick. The Jatte boy and girl might be dangerous, but they would be less adept than the others. The wolfman, catwoman, and four-armed one were unknowns, and an enemy about which you knew nothing was worse than one about which you knew much. Who could say what those three might be able to do? He had seen evidence of their superior eyes and ears during the night, and that alone gave him pause.

Fosull nearly tripped on a rock, so intent was he on his thoughts. Careful, fool! It would hardly do to fall and break a leg while planning how to best so many enemies.

The truce declared with Raseri for the rescue of Vilken and the Jatte children was finished, Fosull felt. If all this group died and went straight to the Green Pit, it would bother Fosull not the slightest. If they survived those chasing them, Fosull would certainly try to see that such a thing happened, could he do it with minimal risk. It would be a pity to ruin so much meat; still, they could not reasonably be expected to carry it back on foot before it spoiled, and better that Raseri and his were dead and spoiled here than alive to kill Vargs again someday.

One had to look after one's own kind first, after all.

Conan reached the rocks ahead of the others and began looking for ways to slow their pursuers. A kind of animal trail would through the smaller rocks and into a two-span-wide cleft between two high walls of the reddish stone.

As dawn pushed the sun into the sky, Conan began to climb the wall to the right, scrambling up it with a skill born of long practice as a boy in Cimmeria. The height was perhaps five times his own, and it was but the work of a few moments to scale the small peak and achieve the top.

In the gathering light of early morn, he could see the horses and men in the distance, still perhaps half an hour's travel away.

Conan looked around.

"Ho, Conan! What are you about?" That from Penz.

He leaned over and saw the others below in the cleft.

"A surprise for our friends behind us. Can you climb up here and bring your rope?"

"Aye."

When Penz arrived, Conan had already begun moving boulders to the lip of the short peak's edge. He had balanced several large rocks into a precarious pile, held in place by small shards propped against one side.

"Do you have enough line to reach from here to the ground and across the patch?"

"Aye, twice that."

"Measure it out."

Penz did so, and Conan drew his sword and cut the thin hemp. He tied the end around several of the rock shard supports and carefully dropped the rest of the line into the cleft, keeping the weight of it from pulling on the props.

"Best all of you below move ahead and out of the way," Conan called.

For the next few moments Conan and Penz moved more rocks to rest along the lip, leaning them against each other and the first pile. Twice small stones rolled over the edge and threatened to unbalance the collection, but both times Conan or Penz managed to stop it from happening.

"They will be here in a few moments," Conan said, glancing back at their pursuers. "Let us climb down and prepare."

Quickly the two men did just that. At the bottom of the cleft, Conan wrapped the rope around a rock resting in a deep shadow and strung the rest of the rope across the cleft a span above. With luck, a man or a horse would not see it in time to avoid tripping on it.

Vilken returned, sent by his father to report to Conan.

"The path winds higher into the rocks," he said. "There is another high stretch of flat ground past these outcrops, and then the foothills. My father says that if we can make it that far, the horses will not be able to follow us."

Conan nodded. "Good. If we can be certain of delaying them here, then they will not be able to catch us on foot."

Penz looped the reminder of his rope into a coil that he placed over his shoulder and across his chest. "What if they realize that they can circle these rocks and thus avoid our trap?"

"We shall have to make certain that they do not," Conan said.

"And how do we do that?"

"You go and join the others. I shall stay behind to give them something to chase."

Penz nodded, his wolfish features expressionless. "Take care, Conan. Dake wants the rest of us alive, I would wager, but like as not he would see you dead."

"Not to worry, friend. Cimmerians are taught to be fleet of foot should the need arise. I shall rejoin you shortly."

After Vilken and Penz departed, Conan moved back through the cleft, taking care to avoid the rope strung across the bottom, to stand near the far entrance.

He would not have long to wait.

Dake and Capeya rode in the middle of the phalanx, with mounted and foot troops both before and after them. The morning's light found them nearing a stand of large rocks and hillocks.

" 'Twill be rough going for the horses here," the merchant said. "Better we should circle around. Likely they are headed for yon foothills beyond."

"Could they not have hidden themselves in the rocks, hoping we would pass?"

"Unlikely. Our tracker would notice the lack of prints on the other side, and then they would be neatly trapped. We have enough men to encircle the rocks, and a few well-placed arrows would fell anyone foolish enough to try to flee. 'Twould be a stupid move on their part to try to hide there."

"Wishful thinking, I suppose," Dake said.

Capeya was about to send a man to tell the leaders of the column to skirt the rocks when Dake heard a yell.

"There they be!"

Dake tightened his knees on the back of his steed

and raised himself up a bit. The man yelling was the bumbling tracker, Squinty.

Beyond, at the edge of the rocks, stood Conan. He apparently took notice of the approaching column, for as Dake watched, the barbarian turned and ran into an opening between the tallest two stones.

"After them!" Capeya yelled.

The four lead horsemen began the chase, the hooves of their mounts kicking up sandy dirt as they galloped off in pursuit. Behind them the first ranks of foot troops followed, slower, but at a respectable speed for men in light armor.

Kreg, doubtless eager to be in on the kill, kicked his own mount into motion and sped off after the leaders.

Dake glanced at Capeya, who smiled in return. They were not so foolish as to risk battle themselves when they had paid fighters for the purpose.

Capeya twisted on his mount and called to those troops and horsemen behind him. "Go! Hurry!"

When the last of the troop was past, Capeya and Dake urged their horses forward, but slowly. The men had been given orders to spare the freaks on pain of being beheaded, but the barbarian was fair game, and a nice purse of silver coins would go to the man who returned bearing *his* head. Conan's spirit would surely join those of his ancestors shortly, considering the number of men focused on that end.

Dake and Capeya arrived at the entrance to the cleft just as the first horsemen reached the middle of the passage. Conan was not in sight.

Of a moment, Dake felt a premonition. He glanced upward and saw that the upper right side of the passage was piled high with many loose rocks. A patch of sunlit rock caught the mage's attention. And—what was this?—a rope dangling from the edge across the lighted portion? What would a rope be doing there?

Almost instantly Dake realized the danger.

"Hold!" he bellowed. "It is a trap!"

Too late. Even as he watched, the rope went taut for an instant. Thin shards of rock shot from the top of the cliff, jerked free by somebody in the space below tripping on the other end of the hemp.

Dozens of rocks, ranging from the size of a man's head to four or five times that large, showered down upon the men and horses below. The men could only go forward or backward; there was no escape to either side, and confusion stalled them. Those in back attempted to stop and turn.

One horseman in front whipped his mount into full speed, only to run smack into a tumbling boulder that knocked him from his steed and smashed him into the ground, crushing his head. The horse kept going and escaped.

Dake saw the scene as if time had slowed, moving like syrup on a winter's day.

Two footmen were flattened by one large rock. It made a sound like a dog crunching small bones.

Two more horsemen felt the hard rain and went down, along with their unfortunate mounts. Dake had never heard a horse scream that way.

Squinty found an overhang that spared him, only to have his neck pierced by a splinter the size of a dagger from a stone shattering nearby. Blood spurted from the hole made when he jerked the splinter out, and he fell, turning the ground around him crimson. Squinty's good fortune ran out with his life's blood.

Kreg, who had entered the cleft with the others, leaped from his horse and ran back along the opposite edge from the falling rocks. The gods who look after fools and slackwits must have shifted their intent from Squinty to Kreg, for he came through with nary a scratch upon him.

When the dust had settled, Capeya and Dake counted the toll: six men dead, two others injured badly enough that they would die shortly, three more damaged but able to survive. Three horses had been killed, one more wounded so gravely that it had to be put to the sword.

In one fell swoop their small army had been reduced by a third.

"May all the gods rot you!" Dake yelled after Conan, who was doubtless well away from earshot. When they caught him, Dake intended to have the barbarian flayed, his skin peeled away, and the wounds rubbed with salt until the man died screaming in agony!

But first they had to catch him.

TWENTY-THREE

"**D**id it work?" Teyle asked.

"Aye, it worked," Conan replied.

"How many did you get?" Raseri asked.

"I did not stop to count them."

The group was nearly to the foothills and as yet there was no sign of pursuit. "Perhaps you got them all," Morja offered.

"I would think that unlikely," Fosull said.

"Perhaps they might not continue pursuit," Oren said.

Penz and Tro and Sab looked at each other. Then Penz said, "Dake will come, even if he has to do it alone. He needs to get within only a few spans of a person to use his spell."

"We broke the spell before," Vilken said. "What is to stop us from doing it again?"

"He was distracted," Sab said. "He will make sure we are guarded if he catches us again. It will do little good to break the enchantment only to find a dagger buried in your guts. Besides, he has other spells."

"I do not fear his rain of toads or unreal demon," Vilken said.

"Those are not his only ensorcelments," Tro said softly. "He has others that are not illusions."

"Aye," Penz said. "Of course, most of them are merely for show. He can turn wine or any other liquid into pure water with a green powder. He can also burn flesh with another conjuration, and create blinding flashes of light. We have seen him do all of those."

"Turning wine into water will avail him little," Conan said, touching his sword for emphasis.

"He is a dangerous enemy," Tro said. "He will follow us to the ends of the earth before he admits defeat. We know him."

Conan nodded. "Very well, then. Let us find a place where the advantage is ours and end his threat forever."

Voices rumbled with worry, but Conan cut them off. "I do not intend to spend the rest of my life looking over my shoulder for Dake or anyone else. And since Raseri and Fosull would not have us lead them to where we might find help, then let us attack and win or lose as we will."

"Even if your trap killed half of them, we are still outnumbered," Penz said.

Conan looked at his companions each in turn. "Dake is a threat to us all. Those who know him best say he will never stop hunting them. He has magical talents that can overcome a strong man's will. He already knows where the Jatte and Vargs live. If he loses our trail, what is to stop him from proceeding directly back to the swamp to lie in wait there? Six of you must return there eventually, is this not so?"

None could fault Conan's logic.

Raseri said, "Aye, Conan is correct. We must slay Dake and his dog if we and our kind are to ever rest easy again."

"We might all die," Sab said.

To the four-armed man Conan said, "Is not a clean death better than a life of slavery, subject to Dake's every whim?"

Tro and Sab exchanged quick glances. The cat-woman nodded slightly.

"Aye," Sab said. "We stand with you."

Penz added his voice. "As shall I."

Fosull said, "While there is something to be said for leading them to the swamps and having my warriors slaughter them there, I find that I too agree."

Raseri nodded. "Dake must die. The sooner the better."

"They must leave their horses to follow us into the high hills," Conan said. "If we search carefully for a place we can defend, then the advantage will be ours. Let us proceed."

Though Conan was not the oldest, nor likely the wisest, the others deferred to his lead. He had been battle-tested, and the assemblage knew this. Conan himself was not altogether confident that he could prevail over those who chased them, but he was not averse to giving it the best of his blade to find out. It was a simple choice: Win or lose, live or die, and while the consequences were dire, it was easy enough for him to commit to it. To fight depended upon skills that Conan knew well, and a man could hardly ask for a better way to be tested than to stand or fall on his own ability.

As they moved higher into the hills, Raseri smiled to himself. It was going as well as if he had directed it all himself. As long as Dake, Conan, and the other freaks died, he would be triumphant. How that happened hardly mattered. In battle or by poison, certainly it *would* happen, and soon.

Fosull found that he was not averse to the idea of a battle. The outswamp men were stronger, but they provided larger targets for his spear. He would watch his back, of course, but better to do something than to wander around out here in the center of nowhere forever. The gods would be with him or not, and the gods had always held a certain warmth for him, he knew. Of course his gods were a long way from home, as were the Vargs and the Jatte, but certainly the outswamp men had few others in these hills that they could call upon. And a poisoned spear at close range was difficult to deflect unless a god put his mind to it, Fosull knew. If the leader of the Vargs threw his weapon, one of his enemies would die at the very least.

* * *

Kreg came riding back toward Dake, looking worse for the layers of reddish dust that coated him.

Dake looked at the filthy man. "Yes?"

"They are into the hills. The trail turns rocky and steep and is narrow, even at the start. The horses cannot climb it."

Dake glanced over at Capeya, who was dozing as he rode. Abruptly the merchant awoke. "What? What is it?"

"We shall have to leave the horses soon," Dake said. "And continue the chase on foot."

Capeya waved one hand in a careless gesture. "I was not born mounted. I can walk as fast and as far as any man."

"I did not doubt it."

"It will be dark in a few more hours," Capeya said. "Surely they shall have to stop. My men have torches. We can continue to follow and thus gain upon them."

"You are a clever hunter," Dake said.

"Aye. My quarry seldom escapes."

To Kreg, Dake said, "Go back to the trail and have the troops tether the animals and make a camp. With good Capeya's permission, of course, we can leave a few men to watch the mounts there until we return."

The merchant nodded his assent. Kreg turned his steed and moved off.

"We shall have them soon," Capeya said. "Trapped like squealing boars."

"Of course. But we must take precautions. Boars do not shower boulders on their hunters."

"I take your point."

As the afternoon sun slanted down toward evening, Conan and the others found that for which they had been searching. The trail wound upward and there came a place where the animals who had worn the path sometimes turned and moved up a steeper incline. This narrower path took great care to ascend; more, it would allow no more than one person at a time to move along it. At the top of this incline there jutted out a flat shelf of rock, perhaps the size of a large house, or even a small inn. To clamber from the path onto the flat shelf required a fair amount of ability; what was easy for a mountain goat was more difficult for a man. Were a fair bowman to stand upon the trail below, he might manage to shoot an arrow to reach the ledge, but it would be a near thing.

Conan climbed up to the shelf and examined it. Above, the hill continued to rise steeply for several hundred spans before it crested. There was no apparent way to arrive upon the shelf from another angle without climbing the hill from behind, and that was unlikely on the part of any pursuers. No, the only way was via the path he had just taken, unless one had wings or was willing to travel a day or two to the other side of the hill. With any potential attacker having to come at them single file, and having to worry about sliding backward at the slightest misstep, this spot was as good as they were likely to find.

Conan worked his way back to the trail below.

"Night comes soon," he said. "And there is where we camp." He pointed up at the shelf.

All were in agreement.

"I shall see if I can snare some rabbits or other small game," Conan said. "The rest of you should climb to yon ledge. You might gather some large rocks, in case we have unwelcome visitors."

With the others working their way upward, Conan went to see if he could provide them with some kind of supper.

The small fire was sufficient to sear the two rabbits and three ground squirrels Conan had collected, and while it was hardly a sumptuous meal, it helped calm the rumbling in the otherwise empty bellies of the escapees. There had been several small mountain streams along the climb to cool their thirst, but the game was more than welcome.

The meal was mostly done. Raseri walked to the edge of the cliff to relieve himself. Fosull and Vilken sat near the other end of the shelf, talking quietly. Penz demonstrated rope tricks to the Jatte twins. Tro and Sab huddled together near the hillside.

Teyle sucked the marrow from a bone and tossed the empty shell into the fire. Conan sat next to her, chewing the last bit of gristle from his own portion of roasted rabbit.

"I did not have time to thank you for our escape and for saving my sister's honor," the giantess said.

"It was nothing."

"Nay, it was." She shivered in the night air.

"Are you cold?"

"A little."

Conan moved closer and put one arm as far around Teyle as it would reach. She was a giant, but she was also a woman, and she had banished the aches from his body. He could warm her, at the very least.

As they sat close together, she said, "My father wishes for your death as much as he does for that of Dake."

"Oh?"

"He takes very seriously his belief that the Jatte must stay hidden forever."

"But what of the forgetfulness potion of which he has spoken?"

She shrugged under his encircling arm. "I have never heard of such a thing."

Conan looked to where Raseri stood relieving himself.

Teyle seemed to realize what she had said. "He is the shaman and knows many herbs that I do not, of course. And he has given his word."

Her loyalty to her father was admirable, but Conan's disquiet was not made easier by her statement. He could not help but recall that Raseri would have cheerfully tortured him to death in the name of the "natural philosophy" he practiced. How much was such a man's—albeit he was a giant—honor to be trusted? Trusting Teyle had put him into a cage, after all, and although they had since gone through adventures that made Conan feel as if she could be relied upon, so such thing could be said of Raseri.

Men who took their duty too seriously could be very dangerous, Conan had learned.

Something disturbed the Cimmerian's light slumber. The fire had long since dwindled to cooling embers, emitting only a fitful glow and little smoke, and the flat stretch of rock had cooled under the night's breath as well. No one stirred on the shelf as far as Conan could see. He sat up.

Low and thick clouds hid most of the stars and the moon, and the air was still.

What had awakened him—?

There, below on the trail, farther down the mount, a tiny speck of orange light glimmed. As he watched, he saw more such lights, and he knew them for torches in the distance. They were around several turnings of the trail, probably an hour or more away, but moving steadily.

Conan reached over and shook Teyle awake.

"What—?"

"Our unwelcome guests come. Behold."

Behind him he heard some of the others stirring, roused by his quiet speech to Teyle, or perhaps by some innate sense of danger such as had roused the Cimmerian.

Penz moved closer. "They are either brave or stupid to travel by night in these mountains. The path is dangerous."

Tro walked to the edge of their camp and peered into the darkness. She was back in a moment. "It is too far to see for certain. At least fifteen men on foot. More, perhaps."

"Looks as if your trap collected a few," Penz said.

"Would that it had taken more."

"Now what?" Teyle asked.

"We wait."

"Perhaps with luck they might pass by without seeing us," Morja said.

Her brother added his thoughts: "We could then go back the way we came and steal their horses."

"Nay," Raseri said. "We chose this place for battle. Better we should make certain they know we are here, eh, Conan?"

The Cimmerian had to agree. "Climbing up here in the dark is not likely, so they shall have to wait until light. Meanwhile, when they draw level with us, perhaps another rain of stone might serve us."

There were few loose rocks on the shelf, and most of those were either too small or too large to be of use; still, there were enough fist- or head-sized chunks for all of the party to have several each. Moving as quietly as they could in the dark, they gathered the stones.

"When I give the command, throw your rocks as quickly as you can. Aim for the torches if you can see nothing else. Hold back some of the stones for use when it gets light."

Conan himself held a rock slightly larger than his fist in his right hand, a smaller stone ready in his left. Were they lucky, they might crack a few skulls or knock three or four men off the trail. Any reduction of the attackers would help.

They watched as the enemy climbed higher toward them. Whatever was done, Conan knew it would have to be done quickly. He and his party had little food and almost no water, and a long siege would quickly deplete both. A day or two at most, and things would have to be ended.

One way or another.

TWENTY-FOUR

The torchman walking directly in front of Dake grunted and suddenly took it upon himself to pitch headfirst over the edge of the trail. He screamed as he tumbled down the hill. His torch lay guttering where it fell. What—?

Then Dake realized that the thumps and thuds he heard were caused by things falling onto the trail or bouncing down the side of the hill from above. Hard things, such as, say, rocks.

"They are above us!" Dake screamed. "Take cover!"

Alas, finding cover was easier commanded than accomplished. The hill sloped upward steeply and offered only dirt and rocks. On the opposite side of the precarious trail, the slope was somewhat steeper, and a leap that way risked bouncing to the bottom, a not-inconsiderable distance, and serious injury or death.

A guard shrieked a curse behind Dake as a rock smashed into his leg, knocking it from under him. Dake saw the white of bone in the man's shattered limb gleam in the light of the remaining torches.

Those men carrying said torches must have realized that being bearers of the light made them more visible targets, for the flaming brands were dropped or thrown away in short order, adding darkness to the confusion.

"Idiot!" Capeya screamed, shoving a man who turned to run and slammed instead into the merchant. "I will have you flogged and quartered and—gukk!"

Whatever further punishment the merchant intended dealing the man would never be known, for a rock easily as big as Capeya's head came down smack upon that portion of him and shattered his skull as if it were no more than an egg hammered by a man's fist.

So much for Dake's wealthy patron.

"Set curse you!" Dake yelled into the darkness. He jammed his hand into his belt pouch and pulled forth his Bottle of Lightning. "Cover your eyes!"

With that, Dake spoke two of the three magic words and uncorked the bottle. He hurled it straight up as hard as he could, then yelled out the final word that completed the spell.

Having seen several of the torches fall down the hillside, Conan was pleased with his initial attack. A rock was certainly a useful weapon when utilized correctly. At this distance, it was better than a sword—

Amidst the screams of the wounded and panicked men below, he heard a yell that sounded familiar.

"Cover your eyes!" came the faint cry.

"Was that not Dake? And had not Penz and Tro and Sab said something about a blinding spell?"

Conan had barely time to turn away and shut his eyes before the impossibly bright light seared through even his closed lids. Reflected off the hill, it was still enough to turn everything white and cause spots to dance before the Cimmerian's gaze.

As quickly as it had come, the flash of white blinked out, and when Conan looked again, he found he could see well enough even though the spots persisted.

Others of his party were not so fortunate.

"By the Green God, I cannot see!" Fosull called out.

"Nor can I!" Vilken said.

To a degree, nearly all of the others were affected; some had not heard the cry; some had, but had not understood it in time. Only the four-armed man was able to see as well as Conan, and that because he had used two of his hands to cover his eyes.

Conan hurled another stone, as did Sab, and then they hurried to make certain that none of their comrades moved in the wrong direction and risked a fatal fall.

"Stand still," Conan ordered. "Sab and I shall lead you away from the edge."

* * *

Below, Dake realized that the rain of stone had ceased. After a final pair of rocks bounced down, well past his position, he realized too that his lighting must have blinded the attackers. It was only a temporary loss of vision, a matter of minutes, and likely would not allow him enough time to gather his troops and mount an attack. Even if he knew exactly *where* to attack, he suspected it would not be a simple matter of marching there and capturing his thralls. Not in the dark, in any event.

Someone scrabbled over the path toward him.

"Dake?"

Kreg. Whatever gods favored the fool had not yet withdrawn their protection, so it seemed.

"Is that them?" Kreg asked.

"Unless the rabbits and squirrels of the mountains have taken up rock-throwing."

"What are we to do?"

"At the moment, nothing. They have ceased their attack. Morning arrives shortly. When we can see them, then we can decide what to do about them."

"Ah."

Came the dawn. Dake inched his way from behind the rock that sheltered him and peered up the hill.

There was a ledge some distance above that jutted from the face of the rise, much like the prow of a ship. Although he could not see anyone upon the ledge from this angle, Dake would wager a gold solon against a copper cent that those he sought were perched on top of that shelf.

Going up there to collect them would be a hellish task. The small trail leading that way was narrow, strewn with loose gravel, and steep enough to provide a nasty fall if one slipped. Dake had no intention of trying to climb that while avoiding the rocks that would surely greet such an attempt.

The situation was not to his liking. He had one trump card he could play, and its use entailed a fair amount of risk. Among his untried conjurations was one he had won in a game of dice from a down-on-his-luck magician who said he was from Zingara. This spell would, so the gambler had claimed, levitate something as heavy as an ox to whatever height one desired—yea, even all the way to the moon. Such a claim had seemed farfetched to Dake at the time, but two of the other spells he won from the unlucky wizard had worked as promised, and one of those was the binding spell that had given Dake command of his thralls.

Even if the spell *did* work, there was a drawback: It would do so only once. The magic needed was fairly strong, the Zingaran wizard had said, and once it was sucked from the storehouse of sorcerous energies in the area, it would burn itself out as did a moth flying into a flame.

Could Dake but get close enough, he could again lay his obedience spell on those rogues above; however, he had no desire to go floating upward to become a target for their rocks and spears.

No, the spell was a good idea, but only if he could distract the escapees' attention enough so that he would not be noticed. Were they busy with other things, he could utilize the magic and take them unawares.

Assuming, of course, that the wizard had not lied to him about this levitation.

Once more behind the safety of his rock, Dake removed from his pouch the focus for the floating trick. It was a small bird, carved from some black and heavy wood, with the runes that would loose its power etched upon the bird's breast. Dake studied the runes. Aye, he recalled the words for which the symbols stood. If the magic was sufficiently potent to lift an ox, then it could certainly lift him and his slackwit assistant. He need only keep his quarry busy enough so that they did not notice him.

Well. That could be done.

Dake grinned at the thought. Before the sun reached his midpoint, it would be done!

"What do you see?" Raseri asked.

Conan pulled himself back from the edge of the shelf. An arrow sailed up a span or two past him, but fell back of its own weight. At this distance, to be hit by such a missile would be less damaging than an insect bite; still, they kept shooting.

"They are mostly hidden," the Cimmerian said. "And since they can see our rocks coming down, there is no point in wasting our supply."

The blindness suffered by the group had been temporary, as Penz had assured them it would be, and all could see as well as they had before. Even so, Conan kept them well back from the edge, so that those below could not discern how many of the escapees might be up here.

"Do you think they will try to attack?" This was from Oren, who seemed pleased at the idea.

"Who can say? I would not, in their position. I would wait and try to starve us out. They cannot know if we have food and water, however, and they may not have much of either themselves."

"So we wait, eh?" That from Fosull. "I like that not."

"Nor do I," Conan said. "But sometimes waiting is the best ploy. It allows our enemies opportunity to make a foolish mistake, and it keeps us from doing the same."

"How long—?" began Teyle. She stopped as a wet, plopping sound interrupted her. There came another such sound, and another, and in a moment the air was filled with the cause:

It was raining toads.

Illusions they might be, but they felt real when they struck. A toad thumped onto Conan's neck, and he brushed it away. By Crom, what did Dake hope to gain with this foolishness?

Below, the nine men who were still able to mount an attack looked at Dake as if he had gone mad.

"You want us to climb up that steep hill against the boulders that will certainly be heaved down upon us? This is surely a stupid idea!"

"Aye," said a second man. "They cannot stay there forever. Why not simply camp down here out of range and wait for them to come down?"

Dake shook his head. "Nay, I am not disposed to wait. I have already begun the attack. Behold!"

The nine men looked up to the sky above the shelf; it was dark, and raining what appeared to be dirt clods upon the ridge. One of the clods bounced down the hill.

"You attack them with toads?"

"Aye, and a demon shall lead you up the hill. Observe!"

The mage performed the conjuration, and the gigantic red demon appeared.

The startled nine drew back, muttering to their gods.

"If you can send *that*," said one man, "why would you need us?"

Dake could not fault the man's logic, but he had no time to cater to it. "I have my reasons."

"May be, friend, but our master is dead, and I do not recall him leaving you in command. Even with your tame demon, such an assault would be suicide!"

How had these men suddenly developed such a grasp of tactics? Dake wondered. Before, they had seemed much less clever. Well. No matter. They would attack, like it or not. He had purposely gathered them in close, so that all would be in range of his obedience spell. He had never done nine at once, but as long as they were bunched within the reach of his magic, there was no reason why the spell should not work.

Dake spoke the words quickly, taking care not to mispronounce them.

"Hey, what is that?" one of the men began fearfully. "What are you—?"

He did not finish expressing his qualms. Dake instead completed his incantation, felt the geas take hold of the nine, and said, "Silence, fools!"

A short distance away, outside of his range, Kreg called out, "The toads have stopped falling."

"No matter." A wave of Dake's hand sent the demon lumbering up the hill. Being an illusion, it was unaffected by the steepness of the slope. The demon was a fearsome sight, to be certain, but useless, as those above knew it for what it was. No matter, though.

"You nine go and capture yon escapees, now!"

Against their wishes, the nine troops began their climb.

"The red demon comes," Penz said.

"Do we need fear it?" Fosull asked.

"Nay, Father. It is an illusion."

"Why, then, is Dake sending it?" Conan wondered aloud. "He knows that we know this."

"Perhaps it is to hide those who come behind it," Penz said. "Observe."

All of the group moved to the edge of the shelf and peered down the hill. A loose line of men clambered upward.

"Ready your stones," Conan said.

"This way," Dake said to Kreg. "Hurry!"

"What are we going to do?"

The pair moved along the trail and rounded the next turning.

"Turn so that I may mount you, pig 'a back," Dake commanded.

Kreg looked puzzled, but turned. Dake climbed up onto his assistant's back, the carved bird of levitation clutched in one hand. He wrapped his free arm around Kreg's chest and pressed his knees against the blond man's sides.

"I do not understand."

"We are going up the mountain."

"Not if you think I can carry you."

"Silence, idiot. I will use magic to lift us. As you feel yourself grow lighter, use your hands to move us along the hill. Take care to stay close so that we are not seen. We shall sneak up on them."

"Ah."

Dake spoke the words represented by the inscribed runes, directing the energy into Kreg. For a moment nothing seemed to happen.

"It is working!" Kreg said.

"Of course it is working, fool. Did I not say that it would?"

Despite his speech, Dake felt a sense of amazement as Kreg's feet left the ground and the pair began to float upward as if they were two linked bubbles in a mug of ale.

"Stay close to the hillside!"

Kreg obeyed, pulling them along with his fingertips, much as a man swimming along the bottom of a pond might.

Well, the old wizard had spoken the truth. Would wonders never cease?

* * *

Four of the nine attackers had been driven back by rocks from Conan's well-thewed arm, and the others dodged similar missiles hurled by the Cimmerian's companions.

"Is that all of them?" Fosull asked, as he threw a stone. The rock fell well short of the climbers and bounced harmlessly past them.

"So it would seem," Raseri said.

"I do not see Dake, nor is Kreg apparent," Conan said.

"Perhaps they went over the side last night," Teyle offered.

"Somehow that seems less than likely."

"They would not risk themselves do they survive," Penz said.

"These troops are certainly either brave or stupid," Raseri said as one of his tossed rocks caught one of the men full in the chest and knocked him down the hill.

"Or enspelled," Tro said.

Dake did not know how long the magic would keep them aloft. Long enough to surprise the escapees, he hoped. He was consoled by the knowledge that if the spell failed, they were but a short way above the angled hillside, and that his fall would be cushioned by Kreg's body if they were to come down unexpectedly.

They had risen well above the level of the shelf upon which their quarry stood showering rocks upon the hapless troops. Now they moved almost horizontally to a position that would bring them directly over the shelf.

"Carefully, carefully."

Below, the red demon had arrived at the ledge and stood there snarling ineffectively. The freaks and Conan ignored the illusion, casting rocks through him, and even walking within the space occupied by the creature. Dozens of evaporating toads still hopped about, although they, like the impotent demon, would be gone soon.

"There, move toward that large boulder on the back edge of the shelf."

Kreg did as directed. When they reached the rock, he gripped it tightly. Dake hopped from his back. This action was enough so that Kreg would have floated away had he not been anchored by his clutch upon the rock. Even so, his legs drifted upward.

"H-h-hey!"

"Silence!" Dake hissed.

"B-b-but I am without weight!"

"I'll take care of that in a moment. Stay where you are until I recapture the others."

"B-b-b-but—"

"I said be quiet!"

Dake moved quickly toward the freaks and that cursed barbarian. They were all gathered at the edge, bent on stopping the remaining troops from ascending. A few more steps and he would be close enough to envelop them in his spell. . . .

Some unknown sense warned Conan of danger. He spun, to see Dake coming toward them from behind!

"Behind us!" Conan yelled. "Move apart!"

Even as he yelled, Conan leaped to one side, away from the others.

Dake continued onward, speaking rapidly a language Conan did not know. The others started to spread out. In panic, Oren scooped up and threw a rock at the advancing magician, but it was hardly more than a pebble, no larger than a man's big toe.

Dake recited the final word of his spell, and the invisible net of magic fell upon the freaks. Only Conan was outside the range. "Don't move!" Dake commanded those he had just enthralled. Obediently, they froze into living statues.

Unfortunately, Dake's command could not stop the rock that Oren had tossed. The rock was small, but it came fast and hard and struck the mage square in the mouth. Two of his front teeth shattered and his lip split, gouting blood.

Dake wiped at his injured mouth. No matter. The boy would suffer for that. Later, after he enspelled Conan and had him leap from the ledge to his death!

Dake turned toward his final prey. Conan had drawn his sword and moved as far away as he could, but it would avail him not. Dake began the incantation again.

At the fourth word of the spell that would enslave the barbarian, Dake found that his injury would not allow him to pronounce it. He spat blood and fragments of teeth, but the gap could not be closed sufficiently to allow him to say the word!

* * *

Conan resolved to go to meet his god with his sword swinging. If he moved fast enough, perhaps he could lay the sharp iron on Dake before the spell captured him completely. He took a deep breath as he watched the man opposite him spit blood. He lifted his blade and charged, screaming.

Dake panicked. He dodged Conan's rush and turned to the enthralled freaks.

"Get him! Kill him!" he tried to say. The words came out, "Hithum! Hilluim!"

None of the freaks moved.

"Yaaah!" Dake screamed.

Something was wrong here, Conan realized. He had deliberately overbalanced when he had launched himself at Dake, so that even if he were enspelled, his momentum might carry him through. Only, instead of snaring him in the geas, Dake had merely moved aside.

Conan's rush carried him to the edge of the shelf. He nearly went over and was forced to drop his sword that he might keep his balance. His weapon slid to the lip and dropped, falling only a few spans before sticking up in the hard ground.

The Cimmerian twisted to face his enemy.

Dake had drawn a long knife from his belt, and was backing away.

Why was he not under Dake's spell? Surely he had been close enough? And why had the man pulled a dagger when he had magic at his command?

Conan grinned as he realized the only possible answer. Something *was* wrong with Dake's magic!

"So, slaver, your power has failed."

Dake continued to back away.

Conan moved in, brawny arms held wide, crouched low, inviting a thrust.

Dake lunged, driving the point of his blade at Conan's heart—

Conan twisted away and slammed the heel of his hand against Dake's shoulder. Dake was knocked sideways, but he slashed backward with the dagger, and the tip dug a furrow across Conan's chest—

The Cimmerian took the cut willingly, for that put him in position to drive his fist into the space under Dake's breastbone with all the power he could muster—

Dake's breath exploded out of him in a wheeze that showered Conan with blood from the man's smashed lips. He dropped the dagger—

Conan grabbed Dake as he sagged and lifted him above his head. He turned and took three quick steps toward the edge of the shelf—

"Doah!" Dake yelled. "Doah!"

Conan bent his powerful arms and legs and when he straightened them, threw Dake high into the air—

And over the edge of the shelf.

"Yaaaaahhhhhh!"

The slaver fell a long way before smashing into a flat rock. The scream cut off as if sliced by a sharp blade. The body bounced the rest of the way down the hill, over the trail below, and out of sight.

The four troopers who remained standing on the steep slope shook themselves and stared up at those on the ledge. Abruptly the four must have decided that they had urgent business elsewhere, for they scurried down to the trail below and did not slow when they reached it.

Conan turned back to look at the rest of his party. The death of Dake had released them from ensorcelment. Several of them came forward to congratulate him.

"H-h-help!"

Conan turned to see Kreg floating in the air at the juncture of the ledge and the hillside.

Penz moved, his rope twirling.

Kreg drifted upward, as a bit of thistle rises over a hot fire.

The wolfman threw his rope. The loop rose and settled over Kreg's shoulders, but in his haste to grab the hemp, the lackey knocked the noose up so that it encircled instead his neck.

Kreg made choking sounds but managed to grab the rope above the noose with both hands and thus gain himself some slack.

The wind began to move Kreg away from the face of the hill and out over the edge of the shelf. Conan could see that Penz was being pulled along and nearly lifted from his feet. The Cimmerian ran to assist the wolfman, catching the rope and adding his weight to it. Even so, the tug was strong.

"Pull me down! Pull me down!"

Conan and Penz tried, but they could only manage to move the floating man toward them slightly. He now drifted over the steepest part of the hill below the ledge, where it was very nearly a straight drop.

"Raseri, your assistance," Conan called.

But as the Jatte moved to aid them, whatever magic responsible for holding Kreg aloft chose at that instant to fail. Kreg went from being like a bird on the end of a string to being like an anvil tethered to one. His face was full of surprise as he hurtled past them, hands waving in a futile attempt to regain some kind of balance. That was a mistake, but Conan did not think that keeping his hands on the rope would have helped Kreg much, considering the speed at which he fell. To Conan and Penz's credit, they managed to maintain their hold on the hemp, although it might have been better for Kreg if they had not.

There came a wet crack as Kreg reached the end of his rope. Conan and the wolfman looked at each other as the others went to observe the man who dangled by his neck below them.

Penz grinned wolfishly.

TWENTY-FIVE

Those who had been Dake's thralls the longest were first to make certain that he was indeed dead. Conan arrived as Penz stripped the few belongings from the body and examined them.

"Aside from his wagon and the coins hidden in the strongbox therein, he had little to show for his wickedness," Sab observed.

"And now he has nothing to show for it. I hope some of his victims will be on hand to argue his passage through the Gray Lands on his way to Gehanna," Tro added.

"And what are your plans now that you are free?" Conan asked.

Tro, Sab, and Penz exchanged glances. "Perhaps we shall return and claim Dake's wagon. He has no further need of it and likely none will contest our ownership of it. We might use it to travel to a place where our appearance is not thought so unusual." Penz was speaking. "You are welcome to come with us, friend. Part of the wagon's proceeds rightfully belong to you."

"Nay, I think not. I have my own road to travel. You may have Dake's wagon and money with my blessing." Conan looked up the hill. The four Jatte and two Vargs were still descending toward them. "Tell me, do you think such a place as you seek exists?"

The wolfman, catwoman, and four-armed man shrugged in unison.

Penz looked at Conan. "Who can say? There are stories of an island off the coast of the Western Sea in the Black Kingdom where all manner of oddities live in harmony. Perhaps we shall go there and see if the tales are true. Dake's money will make the trip possible. We can hire our own guards, if need be. Freaks with swordsmen are bothered less than those without."

The Jatte and Vargs arrived just then.

"Is he truly dead?" Vilken asked.

"Aye. Dead as anyone gets."

"Good."

"And our business together is done," Conan said.

"Nay, but not quite," Raseri said.

Conan looked up at the giant.

"You and these others still know where to find the Jatte."

"And the Vargs," Fosull added.

"When we arrive upon the flatlands, I shall prepare the potion of forgetfulness," Raseri said. "After you have drunk of it, you can go on your way."

Conan glanced at Penz, Tro, and Sab. He saw agreement there, though he was not particularly disposed to give up his own memory.

"Very well. We shall travel with you back to where we began climbing the hills."

Raseri smiled, showing his big white teeth.

Alone in the patch of scrub growth near the place where the merchant's horses—now long gone—had been tethered, Raseri gathered *chu* root, leaves of the *hemin* bush, and the bitter, milky stalks of the *pok* weed. To ingest any of the three was worth death; to drink a potion made from all guaranteed it beyond doubt. A single sip from this brew would fell an ox. Raseri intended that each of the four outsiders would drink an entire cupful.

When he returned to where the others had started an afternoon fire and were roasting rabbits, the Jatte was smiling again. He was, he reckoned, clever beyond any of these small men or Vargs.

Conan watched as Vilken and Oren exchanged the secrets of their skills. The Varg demonstrated his expertise with his spear, while the Jatte boy showed the other how best to hurl a rock. Odd how these two had come to find a certain peace with each other. Were it not for their leaders, who knew but that they might learn to live in peace?

As Raseri approached the fire, Conan stepped to

where Penz squatted, chewing on a leg of cooked rabbit.

"Do you know how to work any of the late Dake's magic tricks?"

Penz wiped grease from his mouth with the back of one hand. "Aye. Some. I cannot call the toad rain or the demon. Neither can I bind others to my will, or fly, but I can use the green powder."

Conan looked sharply at Penz, who grinned in return. "Aye, I do not trust the giant one either."

Conan clapped Penz on the shoulder. "Good."

An hour after Raseri had brought the potion to a simmer in a pot he had made from the bowl-like helmet of one of the fallen soldiers, he deemed the substance cooled enough. Using small metal cups taken from the kits of the dead soldiers, Raseri served up four potions of the brew, leaving nearly half of the dark mix in the makeshift pot.

It was Penz who fetched the cups for himself and the others, and it was Penz who surreptitiously sprinkled dashes of green powder into each cup while his back was turned to Raseri.

As soon as Conan, Tro, Sab, and Penz all had the brew in hand, Raseri said, "Drink up, and forget!"

Conan and the others regarded their cups and each other. The Cimmerian stared at the giant, who still stood next to the fire.

"Why do you hesitate? Have I not given you my word that this is harmless, save to your memory of how to find the Jatte?"

"Aye, so you have said," Conan answered. He looked at the murky brown liquid within the metal cup, and as he watched, it sparkled briefly and turned clear, so that he could see the metal shining dully up at him through what he had supposedly just been transformed into water.

Teyle bent and picked up one of the metal cups and dipped it into the pot. "I too shall drink of it, Father, to show them you speak the truth."

"No!" Raseri grabbed the cup from his daughter.

"Do you fear to have your daughter drink the same brew you would have us down?"

Raseri glared at Conan, then at the others.

"Conan speaks for us," Tro said.

Raseri looked as if he might scream, or attack them, so angry did his face appear. Then it calmed. "Nay, I have no such fear. Though I would save my own memories, observe!"

With that, he put the cup to his lips, tilted it back and drained it, swallowing the contents with one gulp.

Fosull danced toward the fire, snatched up a cup, and dipped it onto the brew. "No one shames a Varg," he said. He swallowed the contents nearly as quickly as had Raseri.

"Gah, what a vile taste," he said. "But now keep your part of the bargain, outswamp men!"

Conan looked at his three friends, and nodded. They drank.

When they were done, Raseri turned away and vomited violently.

"What is this?" Fosull asked. "What is this?"

The Jatte finished emptying his belly, then turned back to face the others.

"Father—?"

"The potion was poisoned," Conan said.

"Father!"

"Aye. And I thought they might demand that I drink of it, so I swallowed oil from the *brill* vine earlier to coat my stomach so none of it would be absorbed. But it is too late for them; already the poison courses through their systems and they will be dead in a matter of a few heartbeats. The secret of the Jatte is once again safe."

Fosull's green skin seemed three shades paler than normal. He dropped to his knees, making a gargling sound. Since he was much smaller than Raseri, Conan figured that the poison would claim him faster.

"You poisoned *me*? We are allies!"

"Do not be any more stupid than you are, Varg," Raseri said. "You are no more than an animal. You would have killed me at the first opportunity."

"True, Jatte. I would have." He grinned weakly. "Still, I will not go to my long sleep alone." And with that, he cast his spear.

Raseri dodged, and the spear only nicked his arm in passing. He put his hand over the small cut and pressed the flesh to stanch the tiny flow of blood.

"You are wrong yet again, Varg. You die with none but these small men to keep you company!"

Vilken had dropped his own spear and rushed to grab his father.

As his son clutched at him, Fosull began counting aloud.

"—three . . . four . . . five . . ."

"What is he doing?" Teyle asked.

"—eight . . . nine . . . ten!"

"The poison has affected his mind," Raseri said.

"Nay," Fosull said, the sickly grin in place, pointed teeth grinning. "I wished only to be certain you did not try to express *my* poison from *your* wound before it had a chance to work."

"What?!"

"Aye. Giltberry juice. See you in Gehanna, Jatte!"

Raseri lifted his hand from the tiny wound and saw that already the edges of the cut had turned black. His legs wobbled and he sat upon the ground, hard. "I die, but I managed to keep the Jatte's secret! You all drank my poison and will follow me quickly!"

Teyle knelt next to her father and held him to her. "Father!"

Conan shook his head. "Nay, Raseri. Your treachery served you not. What we drank was no more than water, your poisoned brew having been altered by Dake's magic, courtesy of Penz."

Raseri's eyes widened in horror as he heard this.

Fosull fell forward onto the ground and died.

A moment later Raseri collapsed, joining the Varg in death.

"I am sorry it had to end this way," Conan said to Teyle. They had built a huge pyre upon which Raseri and Fosull's remains now burned brightly to greet the fall of night.

"He brought it upon himself," Teyle said.

"What will you do now?"

"I am now leader of the Jatte," she said. "I must return and take care of my people."

"And what of us?"

"You mean us no harm. Go your own way."

"And what of the Vargs?"

"Perhaps Vilken and I can make a truce. Too many of our people die for the wrong reasons. There must be a better way."

Conan nodded.

"And what of you, Conan?"

"I am bound for Shadizar. After a long and twisted path, it seems I am finally about to arrive there."

"I wish you good fortune."

"My thanks."

But as Teyle walked closer to the pyre where her father's corpse burned, Conan wondered about Shadizar. After his adventures of the past few months and years, being a thief was going to seem altogether . . . well, altogether dull.

THE DRAGON REBORN

sequel to *The Great Hunt*

Book Three
~of~
The Wheel
of Time

by

Robert Jordan

Praise for *Eye of the World*

"A powerful vision of good and evil...fascinating people moving through a rich and interesting world." —Orson Scott Card

"Richly detailed...fully realized, complex adventure."
—*Library Journal*

"A combination of Robin Hood and Stephen King that is hard to resist...Jordan makes the reader care about these characters as though they were old friends." —*Milwaukee Sentinel*

Praise for *The Great Hunt*

"Jordan can spin as rich a world and as event-filled a tale as [Tolkien]...will not be easy to put down." —*ALA Booklist*

"Worth re-reading a time or two." —*Locus*

"This is good stuff...Splendidly characterized and cleverly plotted...The Great Hunt is a good book which will always be a good book. I shall certainly [line up] for the third volume."
—*Interzone*

The Dragon Reborn
coming in hardcover in August, 1991

THE MIGHTY ADVENTURES OF CONAN

☐ ☐	55210-5	**CONAN THE BOLD** *John Maddox Roberts*	$3.95 Canada $4.95
☐ ☐	50094-6	**CONAN THE CHAMPION** *John Maddox Roberts*	$3.95 Canada $4.95
☐ ☐	51394-0	**CONAN THE DEFENDER** *Robert Jordan*	$3.95 Canada $4.95
☐ ☐	54264-9	**CONAN THE DEFIANT** *Steve Perry*	$6.95 Canada $8.95
☐ ☐	50096-2	**CONAN THE FEARLESS** *Steve Perry*	$3.95 Canada $4.95
☐ ☐	50998-6	**CONAN THE FORMIDABLE** *Steve Perry*	$7.95 Canada $9.50
☐ ☐	50690-1	**CONAN THE FREE LANCE** *Steve Perry*	$3.95 Canada $4.95
☐ ☐	50714-2	**CONAN THE GREAT** *Leonard Carpenter*	$3.95 Canada $4.95
☐ ☐	50961-7	**CONAN THE GUARDIAN** *Roland Green*	$3.95 Canada $4.95
☐ ☐	50860-2	**CONAN THE INDOMITABLE** *Steve Perry*	$3.95 Canada $4.95
☐ ☐	50997-8	**CONAN THE INVINCIBLE** *Robert Jordan*	$3.95 Canada $4.95

Buy them at your local bookstore or use this handy coupon:
Clip and mail this page with your order.

Publishers Book and Audio Mailing Service
P.O. Box 120159, Staten Island, NY 10312-0004

Please send me the book(s) I have checked above. I am enclosing $ _____
(please add $1.25 for the first book, and $.25 for each additional book to cover postage and handling.
Send check or money order only—no CODs).

Name _____
Address _____
City _____ State/Zip _____

Please allow six weeks for delivery. Prices subject to change without notice.

Robert Jordan's
THE EYE OF THE WORLD

The acclaimed first volume of
The Wheel of Time

"This one is as solid as a steel blade, and glowing with the true magic. Robert Jordan deserves congratulations."
—Fred Saberhagen

"The next major fantasy epic!" —Piers Anthony

"A splendid epic of heroic fantasy, vast in scope, colorful in detail, and convincing in its presentation of human character and personality."
—L. Sprague de Camp

☐ 51181-6

$5.95
Canada $6.95